A Cigarette-Maker's Romance

by

F. Marion Crawford

Double9
BOOKS

A Cigarette-Maker's Romance
by F. Marion Crawford

ISBN: 978-93-73407-03-6

Published by

DOUBLE 9 BOOKS
2/13-B, Ansari Road
Daryaganj, New Delhi – 110002
info@double9books.com
www.double9books.com
Tel. 011-40042856

ABOUT THE AUTHOR

Francis Marion Crawford was an American writer best known for his numerous books, particularly those set in Italy, as well as his famous odd and magical stories. Crawford was born in Bagni di Lucca, Grand Duchy of Tuscany, on August 2, 1854. He was the only son of Thomas Crawford, an American sculptor, and Louisa Cutler Ward. His sister was writer Mary Crawford Fraser (also known as Mrs. Hugh Fraser), and he was the nephew of American poet Julia Ward Howe. Following his father's death in 1857, his mother remarried Luther Terry, with whom she bore Crawford's half-sister, Margaret Ward Terry, who eventually married Winthrop Astor Chanler. He attended St Paul's School in Concord, New Hampshire, followed by Cambridge University, the University of Heidelberg, and the University of Rome. In 1879, he traveled to India, where he studied Sanskrit and worked as an editor for the Allahabad Indian Herald. After returning to America in February 1881, he spent a year studying Sanskrit at Harvard University and two years contributing to numerous publications, most notably The Critic. Early in 1882, he formed a long-time acquaintance with Isabella Stewart Gardner.

CONTENTS

CHAPTER I

The inner room of a tobacconist's shop is not perhaps the spot which a writer of fiction would naturally choose as the theatre of his play, nor does the inventor of pleasant romances, of stirring incident, or moving love-tales feel himself instinctively inclined to turn to Munich as to the city of his dreams. On the other hand, it is by no means certain that, if the choice of a stage for our performance were offered to the most contented among us, we should be satisfied to speak our parts and go through our actor's business upon the boards of this world. Some would prefer to take their properties, their player's crowns and robes, their aspiring expressions and their finely expressed aspirations before the audience of a larger planet; others, perhaps the majority, would choose, with more humility as well as with more common sense, the shadowy scenery, the softer footlights and the less exigent public of a modest asteroid, beyond the reach of our earthly haste, of our noisy and unclean high-roads to honour, of our furious chariot races round the goals of fame, and, especially, beyond the reach of competition. But we have no choice. We are in the world and, before we know where we are, we are on one of the paths which we must traverse in our few score years between birth and death. Moreover, each man's path leads up to the theatre on the one side and down from it on the other. The inexorable manager, Fate, requires that each should go through with his comedy or his drama, if he be judged worthy of a leading part, with his scene or his act in another man's piece, if he be fit only to play the walking gentleman, the dumb footman, or the mechanically trained supernumerary who does duty by turns as soldier, sailor, courtier, husbandman, conspirator or red-capped patriot. A few play well, many play badly, all must appear and the majority are feebly applauded and loudly hissed. He counts himself great who is received with such an uproar of clapping and shout of approval as may drown the voice of the discontented; he is called fortunate who, having missed his cue and broken down in his words, makes his exit in the triumphant train of the greater actor upon whom all eyes are turned; he is deemed happy who, having offended no man, is allowed to depart in peace upon his downward road. Yet none of these players need pride themselves much upon their success nor take to heart their failure. Long before most of them have slipped into the grave which waits at the foot of the hill, and have been wrapped comfortably in the pleasant earth, their names are forgotten by those who screamed with pleasure or hooted in disgust at their performance, their faces are no longer remembered, their great drama is become an old-fashioned mummery of the past. Why should they care? Their work is done, they have been rewarded or punished, paid with praise and gold or mulcted in the sum of their reputation and estate. Famous or infamous, in honour or in disrepute, in riches or in poverty, they have reached the end of their time, they are worn out, the world will have no more of them, they are worthless in the price-scale of men, they must be buried out of sight and they will be forgotten out of mind. The beginning is the same for all, and the end also, and as for the future, who shall tell us upon what basis of higher intelligence our brief passage across the stage is to be judged? Why then should the present trouble our vanity so greatly? And if our play is of so little importance, why should we care whether the scenery is romantic instead of commonplace, or why should we make furious efforts to shift a Gothic castle, a drawbridge, a moat and a waterfall into the slides occupied by the four walls of a Munich tobacconist's shop?

There is not even anything especial in the appearance of the place to recommend it to the ready pen of the word-painter. It is an establishment of very modest pretensions situated in one of the side streets leading to a great thoroughfare. As we are in Munich, however, the side street is broad and clean, the pavement is well swept and the adjoining houses have an air of solid respectability and wealth. At the point where the street widens to an irregular shape on the downward slope there is a neat little iron kiosque completely covered with brilliant advertisements, printed in black Gothic letters upon red and yellow paper. The point of vivid colour is not disagreeable, for it relieves the neutral tints of brick and brown stone, and arrests the eye, long wearied with the respectable parade of buildings. The tobacconist's shop is, indeed, the most shabby, or, to speak more correctly, the least smartly new among its fellow-shops, wherein dwell, in consecutive order, a barber, a watchmaker, a pastry-cook, a shoemaker and a colour-man. In spite of its unattractive exterior, however, the establishment of "Christian Fischelowitz, from South Russia," enjoys a very considerable reputation. Within the high, narrow shop there is good store of rare tobaccos, from the mild Kir to the Imperial Samson, the aromatic Dubec and the pungent Swary. The dusty window beside the narrow door exhibits, it is true, only a couple of tall, dried tobacco plants set in flower-pots, a carelessly arranged collection of cedar and pasteboard boxes for cigars and cigarettes, and a fantastically constructed Swiss cottage, built entirely of cigarettes and fine cut yellow leaf, with little pieces of glass set in for windows. This effort of architecture is in a decidedly ruinous condition, the little stuffed paper cylinders are ragged and torn, some of them show signs of detaching themselves from the cardboard frame upon which they are pasted, and the dust of years has accumulated upon the bit of painted board which serves as a foundation for the chalet. In one corner of the window an object more gaudy but not more useful attracts the eye. It is the popular doll figure commonly known in Germany as the "Wiener Gigerl" or "Vienna fop." It is doubtful whether any person could appear in the public places of Vienna in such a costume without being stoned or otherwise painfully put to a shameful death. The doll is arrayed in black shorts and silk stockings, a wide white waistcoat, a scarlet evening coat, an enormous collar and a white tall hat with a broad brim. He stands upon one foot, raising the other as though in the act of beginning a minuet; he holds in one hand a stick and in the other a cigarette, a relatively monstrous eye-glass magnifies one of his painted eyes and upon his face is such an expression of combined insolence, vulgarity, dishonesty and conceit as would insure his being shot at sight in any Western American village making the least pretence to self-respect. On high days and holidays Christian Fischelowitz inserts a key into the square black pedestal whereon the doll has its being, and the thing lives and moves, turns about and cocks its impertinent head at the passers-by, while a feeble tune of uncertain rhythm is heard grating itself out upon the teeth of the metal comb in the concealed mechanism. Fischelowitz delights in this monstrosity, and is never weary of watching its detestable antics. It is doubtful whether in the simplicity of his good-natured heart he does not really believe that the Wiener Gigerl may attract a stray customer to his counter and, in the long-run, pay for itself. For it cost him money, and in itself, as a thing of beauty, it hardly covers the bad debt contracted with him by a poor fellow-countryman to whom he kindly lent fifty marks last year. He accepted the doll without a murmur, however, in full discharge of the obligation, and with an odd philosophy peculiar to himself, he does his best to get what amusement he can out of the little red-coated figure without complaining and without bitterness.

Christian's wife, his larger if not his better half, is less complacent. In the publicity of the shop her small black eyes cast glances full of hate upon the innocent Gigerl, her full flat face reddens with anger when she remembers the money, and her fat hands would dash the insolent little figure into the street, if her mercantile understanding did not suggest the possibility of ultimately selling it for something. In view of such a fortunate contingency, and whenever she is alone, she carefully dusts the thing and puts it away in the cupboard in the corner, well knowing that Fischelowitz will return in an hour, will take it out, set it in its place, wind it up and watch its performance with his everlasting, good-humoured, satisfied smile. In public she ventures only to abuse the doll. In the silent watches of the night she directs her sharp speeches at Christian himself. Not that she is altogether miserly, nor by any means an ill-disposed person. Had she been of such a disposition her husband would not have married her, for he is a very good man of business and a keen judge of other wares besides tobacco. She is a good mother and a good housewife, energetic, thrifty, and of fairly even temper; but that particular piece of generosity which resulted in the acquisition of a red-coated puppet in exchange for fifty marks fills her heart with anger and her plump brown fingers with an itching desire to scratch and tear something or somebody as a means of satisfying her vengeance. For the poor fellow-countryman was one of the Count's friends, and Akulina Fischelowitz abhors the Count and loathes him, and the Wiener Gigerl was the beginning of the end.

While Christian is watching his doll, and Akulina is seated behind the counter, her hands folded upon her lap, and her eyes darting unquiet glances at her husband, the Count is busily occupied in making cigarettes in the dingy back shop among a group of persons, both young and old, all similarly occupied. It is not to be expected that the workroom should be cleaner or more tastefully decorated than the counting-house, and in such a business as the manufacture of cigarettes by hand litter of all sorts accumulates rapidly. The "Famous Cigarette Manufactory of Christian Fischelowitz from South Russia" is about as dingy, as unhealthy, as untidy, as dusty a place as can be found within the limits of tidy, well-to-do Munich. The room is lighted by a window and a half-glazed door, both opening upon a dark court. The walls, originally whitewashed, are of a deep rich brown, attributable partly to the constant fumes and exhalations of tobacco, partly to the fine brown dust of the dried refuse cuttings, and partly to the admirable smoke-giving qualities of the rickety iron stove which stands in one corner, and in which a fire is daily attempted during more than half the year. There are many shelves upon the walls too, and the white wood of these has also received into itself the warm, deep colour. Upon two of these shelves there are accumulations of useless articles, a cracked glass vase, once the pride of the show window, when it was filled to overflowing with fine cut leaf, a broken-down samovar which has seen tea-service in many cities, from Kiew to Moscow, from Moscow to Vilna, from Vilna to Berlin, from Berlin to Munich; there are fragments of Russian lacquered wooden bowls, wrecked cigar-boxes, piles of dingy handbills left over from the last half-yearly advertisement, a crazy Turkish narghile, the broken stem of a chibouque, an old hat and an odd boot, besides irregularly shaped parcels, wrapped in crumpled brown paper and half buried in dust. Upon the other shelves are arranged more neatly rows of tin boxes with locks, and reams of still uncut cigarette paper, some white, some straw-coloured.

Round about the room are the seats of the workers. One man alone is standing at his task, a man with a dark, Cossack face, high cheek-bones, honest, gleaming black eyes, straggling hair and ragged beard. In his shirt-sleeves, his arms bare to the elbow, he handles the heavy swivel knife, pressing the package of carefully arranged leaves forward and under the blade by almost imperceptible degrees. It is one of the most delicate operations in the art, and the man has an especial gift for the work. So sensitive is his strong right hand that as the knife cuts through the thick pile he can detect the presence of a scrap of thin paper amongst the tobacco, and not a bit of hardened stem or a twisted leaf escapes him. It is very hard work, even for a strong man, and the moisture stands in great drops on his dark forehead as he carefully presses the sharp instrument through the resisting substance, quickly lifts it up again and pushes on the package for the next cut.

At a small black table near by sits a Polish girl, poorly dressed, her heavy red-brown hair braided in one long neat tress, her face deadly white, her blue eyes lustreless and sunken, her thin fingers actively rolling bits of paper round a glass tube, drawing them off as the edges are gummed together, and laying them in a prettily arranged pile before her. She is Vjera, the shell-maker, invariably spoken of as "poor Vjera." Vjera, being interpreted from the Russian, means "Faith." There is an odd and pathetic irony in the name borne by the sickly girl. Faith—faith in what? In shell-making? In Christian Fischelowitz? In Johann Schmidt, the Cossack tobacco-cutter, whose real name is lost in the gloom of many dim wanderings? In life? In death? Who knows? In God, at least, poor child—and in her wretched existence there is little else left for her to believe in. If you ask her whether she believes in the Count, she will turn away rather hastily, but in that case the wish to believe is there.

Beside Vjera sits another girl, less pale perhaps, but more insignificant in feature, and similarly occupied, with this slight difference that the little cylinders she makes are straw-coloured when Vjera is making white ones, and white when her companion is using straw-coloured paper. On the opposite side of the room, also before small black tables, sit two men, to wit, Victor Ivanowitch Dumnoff and the Count. It is their business to shape the tobacco and to insert it into the shells, a process performed by rolling the cut leaf into a cylinder in a tongue-shaped piece of parchment, which, when ready, has the form of a pencil, and is slipped into the shell. The parchment is then withdrawn, and the tobacco remains behind in its place; the little bunch of threads which protrudes at each end is cut off with sharp scissors and the cigarette is finished.

The Count, on the afternoon of the day on which this story opens, was sitting before his little black table in his usual attitude, his head stooping slightly forward, his elbows supported on each side of him, his long fingers moving quickly and skilfully, his greyish blue eyes fixed intently on his work. At five o'clock in the afternoon on Tuesday, the sixth of May, in the present year of grace one thousand eight hundred and ninety, the Count was rapidly approaching the two-thousandth cigarette of that day's work. Two thousand in a day was his limit; and though he boasted that he could make three thousand between dawn and midnight, if absolutely necessary, yet he confessed that among the last five hundred a few might be found in which the leaves would be too tightly rolled or too loosely packed. Up to his limit, however, he was to be relied upon, and not one of his hundred score of cigarettes would be found to differ in weight from another by a single grain.

It is perhaps time to describe the outward appearance of the busy worker, out of whose life the events of some six-and-thirty hours furnish the subject of this little tale. The Count is thirty years old, but might be thought older, for there are grey streaks in his smooth black hair, and there is a grey tone in the complexion of his tired face. In figure he is thin, broad shouldered, sinewy, well made and graceful. He moves easily and with a certain elegance. His arms and legs are long in proportion to his body. His head is well shaped, bony, full of energy—his nose is finely modelled and sharply aquiline; a short, dark moustache does not quite hide the firm, well-chiselled lips, and the clean-cut chin is prominent and of the martial type. From under his rather heavy eyebrows a pair of keen eyes, full of changing light and expression, look somewhat contemptuously on the world and its inhabitants. On the whole, the Count is a handsome man and looks a gentleman, in spite of his occupation and in spite of his clothes, which are in the fashion of twenty years ago, but are carefully brushed and all but spotless. There are poor men who can wear a coat as a red Indian will ride a mustang which a white man has left for dead, beyond the period predetermined by the nature of tailoring as the natural term of existence allotted to earthly garments. We look upon a centenarian as a miracle of longevity, and he is careful to tell us his age if he have not lost the power of speech; but if the coats of poor men could speak, how much more marvellous in our eyes would their powers of life appear! A stranger would have taken the Count for a half-pay officer of good birth in straitened circumstances. The expression of his face at the time in question was grave and thoughtful, as though he were thinking of matters weightier to his happiness, if not more necessary to his material welfare than his work. He saw his fingers moving, he watched each honey-coloured bundle of cut leaf as it was rolled in the parchment tongue, and with unswerving regularity he made the motions required to slip the tobacco into the shell. But, while seeing all that he did, and seeing consciously, he looked as though he saw also through the familiar materials shaped under his fingers, into a dim distance full of a larger life and wider interests.

The five occupants of the workshop had been working in silence for nearly half an hour. The two girls on the one side and the two men on the other kept their eyes bent down upon their fingers, while Johann Schmidt, the Cossack, plied his guillotine-like knife in the corner. This same Johann Schmidt, whose real name, to judge from his appearance, might have been Tarass Bulba or Danjelo Buralbash, and was probably of a similar sound, was at once the wit, the spendthrift and the humanitarian of the Fischelowitz manufactory, possessing a number of good qualities in such abundant measure as to make him a total failure in everything except the cutting of tobacco. Like many witty, generous and kind-hearted persons in a much higher rank of existence, he was cursed with a total want of tact. On the present occasion, having sliced through an unusually long package of leaves and having encountered an exceptional number of obstacles in doing so, he thought fit to pause, draw a long breath and wipe the perspiration from his sallow forehead with a pocket-handkerchief in which the neutral tints predominated. This operation, preparatory to a rest of ten minutes, having been successfully accomplished, Tarass Bulba Schmidt picked up a tiny oblong bit of paper which had found its way to his feet from one of the girls' tables, took a pinch of the freshly cut tobacco beside him and rolled a cigarette in his palm with one hand while he felt in his pocket for a match with the other. Then, in the midst of a great cloud of fragrant smoke, he sat down upon the edge of his cutting-block and looked at his companions. After a few moments of deep thought he gave expression to his meditations in bad German. It is curious to see how readily the Slavs in Germany fall into the habit of using the language of the country when conversing together.

"It is my opinion," he said at last, "that the most objectless existences are those which most exactly accomplish the object set before them."

Having given vent to this bit of paradox, Johann inhaled as much smoke as his leathery lungs could contain and relapsed into silence. Vjera, the Polish girl, glanced at the tobacco-cutter and went on with her work. The insignificant girl beside her giggled vacantly. Dumnoff did not seem to have heard the remark.

"Nineteen hundred and twenty-three," muttered the Count between his teeth and in Russian, as the nineteenth hundred and twenty-third cigarette rolled from his fingers, and he took up the parchment tongue for the nineteenth hundred and twenty-fourth time that day.

"I do not exactly understand you, Herr Schmidt," said Vjera without looking up again. "An objectless life has no object. How then—"

"There is nothing to understand," growled Dumnoff, who never counted his own work, and always enjoyed a bit of conversation, provided he could abuse something or somebody. "There is nothing in it, and Herr Schmidt is a Landau moss-head."

It would be curious to ascertain why the wiseacres of eastern Bavaria are held throughout South Germany in such contempt as to be a byword for dulness and stupidity. The Cossack's dark eyes shot a quick glance at the Russian, but he took no notice of the remark.

"I mean," he said, after a pause, "exactly what I say. I am an honest fellow, and I always mean what I say, and no offence to anybody. Do we not all of us, here with Fischelowitz, exactly fulfil the object set before us, I would like to ask? Do we not make cigarettes from morning till night with horrible exactness and regularity? Very well. Do we not, at the same time, lead an atrociously objectless existence?"

"The object of existence is to live," remarked Dumnoff, who was fond of cabbage and strong spirits, and of little else in the world. The Cossack laughed.

"Do you call this living?" he asked contemptuously. Then the good-humoured tone returned to his voice, and he shrugged his bony shoulders as he crossed one leg over the other and took another puff.

"Nineteen hundred and twenty-nine," said the Count.

"Do you call that a life for a Christian man?" asked Schmidt again, looking at him and waving towards him the lighted cigarette he held. "Is that a life for a gentleman, for a real Count, for a noble, for an educated aristocrat, for a man born to be the heir of millions?"

"Thirty," said the Count. "No, it is not. But there is no reason why you should remind us of the fact, that I know of. It is bad enough to be obliged to do the thing, without being made to talk about it. Not that it matters to me so much to-day as it did a year ago, as you may imagine. Thirty-one. It will soon be over for me, at least. In fact I only finish these two thousand out of kindness to Fischelowitz, because I know he has a large order to deliver on the day after to-morrow. And, besides, a gentleman must keep his word even—thirty-two—in the matter of making cigarettes for other people. But the work on this batch shall be a parting gift of my goodwill to Fischelowitz, who is an honest fellow and has understood my painful situation all along. To-morrow at this time, I shall be far away. Thirty-three."

The Count drew a long breath of relief in the anticipation of his release from captivity and hard labour. Vjera dropped her glass tube and her little pieces of paper and looked sadly at him, while he was speaking.

"By the by," observed the Cossack, "to-day is Tuesday. I had quite forgotten. So you really leave us to-morrow."

"Yes. It is all settled at last, and I have had letters. It is to-morrow—and this is my last hundred."

"At what time?" inquired Dumnoff, with a rough laugh. "Is it to be in the morning or in the afternoon?"

"I do not know," answered the Count, quietly and with an air of conviction. "It will certainly be before night."

"Provided you get the news in time to ask us to the feast," jeered the other, "we shall all be as happy as you yourself."

"Thirty-four," said the Count, who had rolled the last cigarette very slowly and thoughtfully.

Vjera cast an imploring look on Dumnoff, as though beseeching him not to continue his jesting. The rough man, who might have sat for the type of the Russian mujik, noticed the glance and was silent.

"Who is incredulous enough to disbelieve this time?" asked the Cossack, gravely. "Besides, the Count says that he has had letters, so it is certain, at last."

"Love-letters, he means," giggled the insignificant girl, who rejoiced in the name of Anna Schmigjelskova. Then she looked at Vjera as though afraid of her displeasure.

But Vjera took no notice of the silly speech and sat idle for some minutes, gazing at the Count with an expression in which love, admiration and pity were very oddly mingled. Pale and ill as she looked, there was a ray of light and a movement of life in her face during those few moments. Then she took again her glass tube and her bits of paper and resumed her task of making shells, with a little heave of her thin chest that betrayed the suppression of a sigh.

The Count finished his second thousand, and arranged the last hundreds neatly with the others, laying them in little heaps and patting the ends with his fingers so that they should present an absolutely symmetrical appearance. Dumnoff plodded on, in his peculiar way, doing the work well and then carelessly tossing it into a basket by his side. He was capable of working fourteen hours at a stretch when there was a prospect of cabbage soup and liquor in the evening. The Cossack cleaned his cutting-block and his broad swivel knife and emptied the cut tobacco into a clean tin box. It was clear that the day's work was almost at an end for all present. At that moment Fischelowitz entered with jaunty step and smiling face, jingling a quantity of loose silver in his hand. He is a little man, rotund and cheerful, quiet of speech and sunny in manner, with a brown beard and waving dark hair, arranged in the manner dear to barbers' apprentices. He has very soft brown eyes, a healthy complexion and a nose the inverse of aquiline, for it curves upwards to its sharp point, as though perpetually snuffing after the pleasant fragrance of his favourite "Dubec otborny."

"Well, my children," he said, with a slight stammer that somehow lent an additional kindliness to his tone, "what has the day's work been? You first, Herr Graf," he added, turning to the Count. "I suppose that you have made a thousand at least?"

Fischelowitz possessed in abundance the tact which was lacking in Johann Schmidt, the Cossack. He well knew that the Count had made double the quantity, but he also knew that the latter enjoyed the small triumph of producing twice what seemed to be expected of him.

"Two thousand, Herr Fischelowitz," he said, proudly. Then seeing that his employer was counting out the sum of six marks, he made a deprecating gesture, as though refusing all payment.

"No," he said, with great dignity, and rising from his seat. "No. You must allow me, on this occasion, to refuse the honorarium usual under the circumstances."

"And why, my dear Count?" inquired Fischelowitz, shaking the six marks in one hand and the remainder of his money in the other, as though weighing the silver. "And why will you refuse me the honour—"

The other working people exchanged glances of amusement, as though they knew what was coming. Vjera hid her face in her hands as she rested her elbows on the table before her.

"I must indeed explain," answered the Count. "To-morrow, I shall be obliged to leave you, not to return to the occupation which has so long been a necessity to me in my troubles. Fortune at last returns to me and I am free. I think I have spoken to you in confidence of my situation, once at least, if not more often. My difficulties are at an end. I have received letters announcing that to-morrow I shall be reinstated in my possessions. You have shown me kindness—kindness, Herr Fischelowitz, and, what has been more than kindness to me, you have shown me great courtesy. Every one has not treated the poor gentleman with the same forbearance. But let bygones be bygones. On the occasion of my return to prosperity, permit me to offer you, as the only gift as yet within my means, the result of my last day's work within these walls. You have been very kind, and I thank you very sincerely."

There was a tremor in the Count's voice, and a moisture in his eyes, as he drew himself up in his threadbare decent frock-coat and held out his sinewy hand, stained with the long handling of tobacco in his daily labour. Fischelowitz smiled with uncommon cheerfulness as he grasped the bony fingers heartily.

"Thank you," he said. "I accept. I esteem it an honour to have been of any assistance to you in your temporary annoyances."

Vjera still hid her face. The Cossack watched what was happening with an expression half sad, half curious, and Dumnoff displayed a set of ferocious white teeth as he stupidly grinned from ear to ear.

CHAPTER II

Fischelowitz paid each worker for the day's work, in his quick, cheerful way, and each, being paid, passed out through the front shop into the street. Five minutes later the Count was strolling along the Maximilians-strasse in the direction of the royal palace. As he walked he drew himself up to the full height of his military figure and looked into the faces of the passers in the way with grave dignity. At that hour there were many people abroad, slim lieutenants in the green uniforms of the Uhlans and in the blue coats and crimson facings of the heavy cavalry, superior officers with silver or gold plated epaulettes, slim maidens and plump matrons, beardless students in bright, coloured caps, and solemn, elderly civilians with great beards and greater spectacles, great Munich burghers and little Munich nobles, gaily dressed children of all ages, dogs of every breed from the Saint Bernard to the crooked-jointed Dachs, perambulators not a few and legions of nursery-maids. Most of the people who passed cast a glance at the thoroughbred-looking man in the threadbare frock-coat who looked at them all with such an air of quiet superiority, carrying his head so high and putting down his feet with such a firm tread. There were doubtless those among the crowd who saw in the tired face the indications of a life-story not without interest, for the crowd was not, nor ever is, in Munich, lacking in intelligent and observant persons. But in all the multitude there was not one man or woman who knew the name of the individual to whom the face belonged, and there were few who would have risked the respectability of their social position by making the acquaintance of a man so evidently poor, even if the occasion had presented itself.

But presently a figure was seen moving swiftly through the throng in the direction already taken by the Count, a figure of a type much more familiar to the sight of the Munich stroller, for it was that of a poorly dressed girl with a long plait of red-brown hair, carrying a covered brown straw basket upon one arm and hurrying along with the noiseless tread possible only in the extreme old age of shoes that were never strong. Poor Vjera had been sent by Fischelowitz with a thousand cigarettes to be delivered at one of the hotels. She was generally employed upon like errands, because she was the poorest in the establishment, and those who received the wares gave her a few pence for her trouble. She sped quickly onward, until she suddenly found herself close behind the Count. Then she slackened her pace and crept along as noiselessly as possible, her eyes fixed upon him as she walked and evidently doing her best not to overtake him nor to be seen by him. As luck would have it, however, the Count suddenly stood still before the show window of a picture-dealer's shop. A clever painting of a solitary Cossack riding along a stony mountain road, by Josef Brandt, had attracted his attention. Then as he realised that he had looked at the picture a dozen times during the previous week, his eye wandered, and in the reflection of the plate-glass window he caught sight of Vjera's slight form at no great distance from him. He turned sharply upon his heels and met her eyes, taking off his limp hat with a courteous gesture.

"Permit me," he said, laying his hand upon the basket and trying to take it from her.

Poor Vjera's face flushed suddenly, and her grip tightened upon the straw handle and she refused to let it go.

"No, you shall never do that again," she said, quickly, trying to draw back from him.

"And why not? Why should I not do you a service?"

"The other day you took it—the people stared at you—they never stare at me, for I am only a poor girl—"

"And what are the people or what is their staring to me?" asked the Count, quietly. "I am not afraid of being taken for a servant or a porter, because I carry a lady's parcel. Pray give me the basket."

"Oh no, pray let it be," cried Vjera, in great earnest. "I cannot bear to see you with such a thing in your hand."

They were still standing before the picture-dealer's window, while many people passed along the pavement. In trying to draw away, Vjera found herself suddenly in the stream, and just then a broad-shouldered officer who chanced to be looking the other way came into collision with her, so roughly that she was forced almost into the Count's arms. The latter made a step forward.

"Is it your habit to jostle ladies in that way?" he asked in a sharp tone, addressing the stout lieutenant.

The latter muttered something which might be taken for an apology and passed on, having no intention of being drawn into a street quarrel with an odd-looking individual who, from his accent, was evidently a foreigner. The Count's eyes darted an angry glance after the offender, and then he looked again at Vjera. In the little accident he had got possession of the basket. Thereupon he passed it to his left hand and offered Vjera his right arm.

"Did the insolent fellow hurt you?" he asked anxiously, in Polish.

"Oh no—only give me my basket!" Vjera's face was painfully flushed.

"No, my dear child," said the Count, gravely. "You will not deny me the pleasure of accompanying you and of carrying your burden. Afterwards, if you will, we can take a little walk together, before I see you to your home."

"You are always so kind to me," answered the girl, bending her head, as though to hide her burning cheeks, but submitting at last to his will.

For some minutes they walked on in silence. Then Vjera showed by a gesture that she wished to cross the street, on the other side of which was situated one of the principal hotels of the city. In front of the entrance Vjera put out her hand entreatingly towards her basket, but the Count took no notice of the attempt and resolutely ascended the steps of the porch by her side. Behind the swinging glass door stood the huge porter amply endowed with that military appearance so characteristic of all men in Germany who wear anything of the nature of an official costume.

"The lady has a package for some one here," said the Count, holding out the basket.

"For the head waiter," said Vjera, timidly.

The porter took the basket, set it down, touched the button of an electric bell and silently looked at the pair with the malignant scrutiny which is the prerogative of servants in their manner with those whom they are privileged to consider as their inferiors. Presently, however, meeting the Count's cold stare, he turned away and strolled up the vestibule. A moment later the head waiter appeared, glorious in a perfectly new evening coat and a phenomenal shirt front.

"Ah, my cigarettes!" he exclaimed briskly, and the Count heard the chink of the nickel pence, as the head waiter inserted two fat white fingers into the pocket of his exceedingly fashionable waistcoat.

The sight which must follow was one which the Count was anxious not to see. He therefore turned his back and pretended to brush from his sleeve a speck of dust revealed to his searching eye in the strong afternoon light which streamed through the open door. Then Vjera's low-spoken word of thanks and her light tread made him aware that she had received her little gratuity; he stood politely aside while she passed out, and then went down the half-dozen steps with her. As they began to move up the street, he did not offer her his arm again.

"You are so kind, so kind to me," said poor Vjera. "How can I ever thank you!"

"Between you and me there is no question of thanks," answered her companion. "Or if there is to be such a question it should arise in another way. It is for me to thank you."

"For what?"

"For many things, all of which have proceeded from your kindness of heart and have resulted in making my life bearable during the past months—or years. I keep little account of time. How long is it since I have been making cigarettes for Fischelowitz, at the rate of three marks a thousand?"

"Ever since I can remember," answered Vjera. "It is six years since I came to work there as a little girl."

"Six years? That is not possible! You must be mistaken, it cannot be so long."

Vjera said nothing, but turned her face away with an expression of pain.

"Yes, it is a long time, since all that happened," said the Count, thoughtfully. "I was a young man then, I am old now."

"Old! How can you say anything so untrue!" Vjera exclaimed with considerable indignation.

"Yes, I am old. It is no wonder. We say at home that 'strange earth dies without wind.' A foreign land will make old bones of a man without the help of years. That is what Germany has done for me. And yet, how much older I should be but for you, dear Vjera! Shall we sit down here, in this quiet place, under the trees? You know it is all over to-morrow, and I am free at last. I would like to tell you my story."

Vjera, who was tired of the close atmosphere of the workroom and whose strength was not enough to let her walk far with pleasure, sat down upon the green bench willingly enough, but the nervous look of pain had not disappeared from her face.

"Is it of any use to tell it to me again?" she asked, sadly, as she leaned against the painted backboard.

The Count produced a cigarette and gravely lighted it, before he answered her, and when he spoke he seemed to attach little or no importance to her question.

"You see," he said, "it is all different now, and I can look at it from a different point of view. Formerly when I spoke of it, I am afraid that I spoke bitterly, for, of course, I could not foresee that it could all come right again so soon, so very soon. And now that this weary time is over I can look back upon it with some pride, if with little pleasure—save for the part you have played in my life, and—may I say it?—saving the part I have played in yours."

He put out his hand gently and tenderly touched hers, and there was something in the meeting of those two thin, yellow hands, stained with the same daily labour and not meeting for the first time thus, that sent a thrill to the two hearts and that might have brought a look of thoughtful interest into eyes dulled and wearied by the ordinary sights of this world. Vjera did not resent the innocent caress, but the colour that came into her face was not of the same hue as that which had burned there when he had insisted upon carrying her basket. This time the blush was not painful to see, but rather shed a faint light of beauty over the plain, pale features. Poor Vjera was happy for a moment.

"I am very glad if I have been anything to you," she said. "I would I might have been more."

"More? I do not see—you have been gentle, forbearing, respecting my misfortunes and trying to make others respect them. What more could you have done, or what more could you have been?"

Vjera was silent, but she softly withdrew her hand from his and gazed at the people in the distance. The Count smoked without speaking, for several minutes, closing his eyes as though revolving a great problem in his mind, then glancing sidelong at his companion's face, hesitating as though about to speak, checking himself and shutting his eyes again in meditation. Holding his cigarette between his teeth he clasped his fingers together tightly, unclasped them again and let his arms fall on each side of him. At last he turned sharply, as though resolved what to do.

He believed that he was on the very eve of recovering a vast fortune and of resuming a high position in the world. It was no wonder that there was a struggle in his soul, when at that moment a new complication seemed to present itself. He was indeed sure that he did not love Vjera, and in the brilliant dreams which floated before his half-closed eyes, visions of beautiful and high-born women dazzled him with their smiles and enchanted him by the perfect grace of their movements. To-morrow he might choose his wife among such as they. But to-day Vjera was by his side, poor Vjera, who alone of those he had known during the years of his captivity had stood by him, had felt for him, had given him a sense of reliance in her perfect sincerity and honest affection. And her affection had grown into something more; it had developed into love during the last months. He had seen it, had known it and had done nothing to arrest the growth. Nay, he had done worse. Only a moment ago he had taken her hand in a way which might well mislead an innocent girl. The Count, according to his lights, was the very incarnation of the theory, honour, in the practice, honesty. His path was clear. If he had deceived Vjera in the very smallest accent of word or detail of deed he must make instant reparation. This was the reason why he turned sharply in his seat and looked at her with a look which was certainly kind, but which was, perhaps, more full of determination than of lover-like tenderness.

"Vjera," he said, slowly, pausing on every syllable of his speech, "will you be my wife?"

Vjera looked at him long and shook her head in silence. Instead of blushing, she turned pale, changing colour with that suddenness which belongs to delicate or exhausted organisations. The Count did not heed the plain though unspoken negation and continued to speak very slowly and earnestly, choosing his words and rounding his expressions as though he were making a declaration to a young princess instead of asking a poor Polish girl to marry him. He even drew himself together, as it were, with the movement of dignity which was habitual with him, straightening his back, squaring his shoulders and leaning slightly forward in his seat. As he began to speak again, Vjera clasped her hands upon her knees and looked down at the gravel of the public path.

"I am in earnest," he said. "To-morrow, all those rights to which I was born will be restored to me, and I shall enjoy what the world calls a great position. Am I so deeply indebted to the world that I must submit to all its prejudices and traditions? Has the world given me anything, in exchange for which it becomes my duty to consult its caprices, or its social superstitions? Surely not. To whom am I most indebted, to the world which has turned its back on me during a temporary embarrassment and loss of fortune, or to my friend Vjera who has been faithfully kind all along? The question itself is foolish. I owe everything to Vjera, and nothing to the world. The case is simple, the argument is short and the verdict is plain. I will not take the riches and the dignities which will be mine by this time to-morrow to the feet of some high-born lady who, to-day, would look coldly on me because I am not—not quite in the fashion, so far as outward appearance is concerned. But I will and I do offer all, wealth, title, dignity, everything to Vjera. And she shakes her head, and with a single gesture refuses it all. Why? Has she a reason to give? An argument to set up? A sensible ground for her decision? No, certainly not."

As he looked gravely towards her averted face, Vjera again shook her head, slowly and thoughtfully, with an air of unalterable determination. He seemed surprised at her obstinacy and watched her in silence for a few moments.

"I see," he said at last, very sadly. "You think that I do not love you." Vjera made no sign, and a long pause followed during which the Count's features expressed great perplexity.

The day was drawing to its close and the low sun shot level rays through the trees of the Hofgarten, far above the heads of the laughing children, the gossiping nurses and the slowly moving crowd that filled the pavement along the drive in front of the palace. Vjera and the Count were seated on a bench which was now already in the shade. The air was beginning to grow chilly, but neither of them heeded the change.

"You think that I do not love you," said the Count again. "You are mistaken, deeply mistaken, Vjera."

The faint, soft colour rose in the poor girl's waxen cheeks, and there was an unaccustomed light in her weary blue eyes as they met his.

"I do not say," continued her companion, "that I love you as boys love at twenty. I am past that. I am not a young man any more, and I have had misfortunes such as would have broken the hearts of most men, and of the kind that do not dispose to great love-passion. If my troubles had come to me through the love of a woman—it might have been otherwise. As it is—do you think that I have no love for you, Vjera? Do not think that, dear—do not let me see that you think it, for it would hurt me. There is much for you, much, very much."

"To-day," answered Vjera, sadly, "but not to-morrow."

"You are cruel, without meaning to be even unkind," said the Count in an unsteady voice. This time it was Vjera who took his hand in hers and pressed it.

"God forbid that I should have an unkind thought for you," she said, very tenderly.

The Count turned to her again and there was a moisture in his eyes of which he was unconscious.

"Then believe that I do truly love you, Vjera," he answered. "Believe that all that there is to give you, I give, and that my all is not a little. I love you, child, in a way—ah, well, you have your girlish dreams of love, and it is right that you should have them and it would be very wrong to destroy them. But they shall not be destroyed by me, and surely not by any other man, while I live. I shall grow young again, I will grow young for you, for, in years at least, I am not old. I will be a boy for you, Vjera, and I will love as boys love, but with the strength of a man who has known sorrow and overlived it. You shall not feel that in taking me you are taking a father, a protector, a man to whom your youth seems childhood, and your youthfulness childish folly. No, no—I will be more than that to you, I will be all to you that you are to me, and more, and more, each day, till love has made us of one age, of one mind, of one heart. Do you not believe that all this shall be? Speak, dear. What is there yet behind in your thoughts?"

"I cannot tell. I wish I knew." Vjera's answer was scarcely audible and she turned her face from him.

"And yet, there is something, you are keeping something from me, when I have kept nothing from you. Why is it? Why do you not quite trust me and believe in me? I can make you happy, now. Yesterday it was different and so it was in all the yesterdays of yesterdays. I had nothing to offer you but myself."

"It were best so," said Vjera in a low voice.

The Count was silent. There was something in her manner which he could not understand, or rather, as he fancied, there was something in his own brain which prevented him from understanding a very simple matter, and he grew impatient with himself. At the same time he felt more and more strongly drawn to the young girl at his side. As the sun went down and the evening shadows deepened, he saw more in her face than he had been accustomed to see there. Every line of the pale features so familiar to his sight in his everyday life, reminded him of moments in the recent past when he had been wretchedly unhappy, and when the kindly look in Vjera's face had comforted him and made life seem less unbearable. In his dreary world she alone had shown that she cared whether he lived or died, were insulted or respected, were treated like a dog or like a Christian man. The kindness of his employer was indeed undeniable, but it was of the sort which grated upon the sensitive nature of the unfortunate cigarette-maker, for it was in itself vulgarly cheerful, assuming that, after all, the Count should be contented with his lot. But Vjera had always seemed to understand him, to feel for him, to foresee his sensibilities as it were, and to be prepared for them. In a measure appreciable to himself she admired him, and admiration alone can make pity palatable to the proud. In her eyes his constancy under misfortune was as admirable as his misfortunes themselves were worthy of commiseration. In her eyes he was a gentleman, and one who had a right to hold his head high among the best. When he was poorest, he had felt himself to be in her eyes a hero. Are there many men who can resist the charm of the one woman who believes them to be heroic? Are not most men, too, really better for the trust and faith that is placed in them by others, as the earthen vessel, valueless in itself, becomes a thing of prize and beauty under the loving hand of the artist who draws graceful figures upon it and colours it skilfully, and handles it tenderly?

And now the poor man was puzzled and made anxious by the girl's obstinate rejection of his offer. A chilly thought took shape in his mind and pained him exceedingly.

"Vjera," he said at last, "I see how it is. You have never loved me. You have only pitied me. You are good and kind, Vjera, but I wish it had been otherwise."

He spoke very quietly, in a subdued tone, and the moisture which had been more than once in his eyes since he had sat down beside the young girl, now almost took the shape of a tear. He was wounded in his innocent vanity, in the last stronghold of his fast-fading individuality. But Vjera turned quickly at the words and a momentary fire illuminated her pale blue eyes and dispelled the misty veil that seemed to dull them.

"Whatever you say, do not say that!" she exclaimed. "I love you with all my heart—I—ah, if you only understood, if you only knew, if you only guessed!"

"That is it," answered the Count. "If I only could—but there is something that passes my understanding."

The look of pain faded from his face and gave way to a bright smile, so bright, so rare, that it restored in the magic of an instant the freshness of early youth to the weary mask of sorrow. Then he covered his eyes with his hands as though searching his memory for something he could not find.

"What is it?" he asked, after a short pause and looking suddenly at Vjera. "It is something I ought to remember and yet something I have quite forgotten. Help me, Vjera, tell me what you are thinking of, and I will explain it all."

"I was thinking of this day a week ago," said Vjera, and a little sob escaped her as she quickly looked away.

"A week ago? Let me see—what happened a week ago? But why should I ask? Nothing ever happens to me, nothing until now! And now, oh Vjera, it is you who do not understand, it is you who do not know, who cannot guess."

As if he had forgotten everything else in the sudden realisation of his return to liberty and fortune, he began to speak quickly and excitedly in a tone louder and clearer than that of his ordinary voice.

"No," he cried, "you can never guess what this change is to me. You can never know what I enjoy in the thought of being myself again, you cannot understand what it is to have been rich and great, and to be poor and wretched and to regain wealth and dignity again by the stroke of a pen in the vibration of a second. And yet it is true, all true, I tell you, to-day, at last, after so much waiting. To-morrow they will come to my lodging to fetch me—a court carriage or two, and many officials who will treat me with the old respect I was used to long ago. They will come up my little staircase, bringing money, immense quantities of money, and the papers and the parchments and the seals. How they will stare at my poor lodging, for they have never known that I have been so wretched. Yes, one will bring money in a black leathern case—I know just how it will look—and another will have with him a box full of documents—all lawfully mine—and a third will bring my orders, that I once wore, and with them the order of Saint Alexander Nevsky and a letter on broad heavy paper, signed Alexander Alexandrovitch, signed by the Tsar himself, Vjera. And I shall go with them to be received in audience by the Prince Regent here, before I leave for Petersburg. And then, after dinner, in the evening, I will get into my special carriage in the express train and my servants will make me comfortable and then away, away, a night, and a day and another night and perhaps a few hours more and I shall be at home at last, in my own great, beautiful home, far out in the glorious country among the woods and the streams and the birds; and I shall be driven in an open carriage with four horses up from the village through the great avenue of poplars to the grand old house. But before I go in I will go to the tomb—yes, I will go to the tomb among the trees, and I will say a prayer for my father and—"

"Your father?" Vjera started slightly. She had listened to the long catalogue of the poor man's anticipations with a sad, unchanging face, as though she had heard it all before. But at the mention of his father's death she seemed surprised.

"Yes. He is dead at last, and my brother died on the same day. I have had letters. There was a disease abroad in the village. They caught it and they died. And now everything is mine, everything, the lands and the houses and the money, all, all mine. But I will say a prayer for them, now that they are dead and I shall never see them again. God knows, they treated me ill when they were alive, but death has them at last."

The Count's eyes grew suddenly cold and hard, so that Vjera shuddered as she caught the look of hatred in them.

"Death, death, death!" he cried. "Death the judge, the gaoler, the executioner! He has done justice on them for me, and they will not break loose from the house he has made for them to lie in and to sleep in for ever. And now, friend Death, I am master in their stead, and you must give me time to enjoy the mastership before you serve me likewise. Oh Vjera, the joy, the delight, the ecstasy, the glory of it all!"

He struck the palms of his lean hands together with the gesture of a boy, and laughed aloud in the sheer overflowing of his heart. But Vjera sat still, silent and thoughtful, beside him, watching him rather anxiously as though she feared lest the excess of his happiness might do him an injury.

"You do not say anything, Vjera. You do not seem glad," he said, suddenly noticing her expression.

"I am very glad, indeed I am," she answered, smiling with a great effort. "Who would not be glad at the thought of seeing you enjoy your own again?"

"It is not for the money, Vjera!" he exclaimed in a lower and more concentrated tone. "It is not really for the money nor for the lands, nor even for the position or the dignity. Do you know what it is that makes me so happy? I have got the best of it. That is it. It has been a long struggle and a weary one, but I knew I should win, though I never saw how it was to be. When they turned me away from them like a dog, my father and my brother, I faced them on the threshold for the last time and I said to them, 'Look you, you have made an outcast of me, and yet I am your son, my father, and your brother, my brother, and you know it. And yet I tell you that when we meet again, I shall be master here, and not you.' And so it has turned out, Vjera, for they shall meet me—they dead, and I alive. They jeered and laughed, and sent me away with only the clothes I wore, for I would not take their money. I hear their laughter now in my ears—but I hear, too, a laugh that is louder and more pitiless than theirs was, for it is the laugh of Death!"

CHAPTER III

The Count rose to his feet as he finished the last sentence. It seemed as though he were oppressed by the inaction to which he was constrained during the last hours of waiting before the great moment, and he moved nervously, like a man anxious to throw off a burden.

Vjera rose also, with a slow and weary movement.

"It is late," she said. "I must go home. Good-night."

"No. I will go with you. I will see you to your door."

"Thank you," she answered, watching his face closely.

Then the two walked side by side under the lime trees in the deepening evening shadows, to the low archway by which the road leads out of the Hofgarten on the side of the city. For some minutes neither spoke, but Vjera could hear her companion's quickly drawn, irregular breath. His heart was beating fast and his thoughts were chasing each other through a labyrinth of dreams, inconsequent, unreasonable, but brilliant in the extreme. His head high, his shoulders thrown back, his eyes flashing, his lips tightly closed, the Count marched out with his companion into the broad square. He felt that this had been the last day of his slavery and that the morrow's sun was to rise upon a brighter and a happier period of his life, in which there should be no more poverty, no more manual labour, no more pinching and grinding and tormenting of himself in the hopeless effort at outward and visible respectability. Poor Vjera saw in his face what was passing in his mind, but her own expression of sadness did not change. On the contrary, since his last outbreak of triumphant satisfaction she had been more than usually depressed. For a long time the Count did not again notice her low spirits, being absorbed in the contemplation of his own splendid future. At last he seemed to recollect her presence at his side, glanced at her, made as though to say something, checked himself, and began humming snatches from an old opera. But either his musical memory did not serve him, or his humour changed all at once, for he suddenly was silent again, and after glancing once more at Vjera's downcast face his own became very grave.

He had been brought back to present considerations, and he found himself in one of those dilemmas with which his genuine pride, his innocent and harmless vanity and his innate kindness constantly beset his life. He had asked Vjera to marry him, scarcely half an hour earlier, and he now found himself separated from the moment which had given birth to the generous impulse, by a lengthened contemplation of his own immediate return to wealth and importance.

He was deeply attached to the poor Polish girl, as men shipwrecked upon desert Islands grow fond of persons upon whom they could have bestowed no thought in ordinary life. He had grown well accustomed to his poor existence, and in the surroundings in which he found himself, Vjera was the one being in whom, besides sympathy for his misfortune, he discovered a sensibility rarer than common, and the unconscious development of a natural refinement. There are strange elements to be found in all great cities among the colonies of strangers who make their dwellings therein. Brought together by trouble, they live in tolerance among themselves, and none asks the other the fundamental question of upper society, "Whence art thou?"—nor does any make of his neighbour the inquiry which rises first to the lips of the man of action, "Whither goest thou?" They meet as the seaweed meets on the crest of the wave, of many colours from many distant depths, to intermingle for a time in the motion of the waters, to part company under the driving of the north wind, to be drifted at last, forgetful of each other, by tides and currents which wash the opposite ends of the earth. This is the life of the emigrant, of the exile, of the wanderer among men; the incongruous elements meet, have brief acquaintance and part, not to meet again. Who shall count the faces that the exile has known, the voices that have been familiar in his ear, the hands that have pressed his? In every land and in every city, he has met and talked with a score, with scores, with hundreds of men and women all leading the more or less mysterious and uncertain life which has become his own by necessity or by choice. If he be an honest man and poor, a dozen trades have occupied his fingers in half a dozen capitals; if he be dishonest, a hundred forms and varieties of money-bringing dishonesty are sheathed like arrows in his quiver, to be shot unawares into the crowd of well-to-do and unsuspecting citizens on the borders of whose respectable society the adventurer warily picks his path.

It is rarely that two persons meet under such circumstances between whom the bond of a real sympathy exists and can develop into lasting friendship between man and man, or into true love between man and woman. When both feel themselves approaching such a point, they are also unconsciously returning to civilisation, and with the civilising influence arises the desire to ask the fatal question, "Whence art thou?"—or the fear lest the other may ask it, and the anxiety to find an answer where there is none that will bear scrutiny.

It was therefore natural that the Count should feel disturbed at what he had done, in spite of his sincere and honourable wish to abide by his proposal and to make Vjera his wife. He felt that in returning to his own position in the world he owed it in a measure to himself to wed with a maiden of whom he could at least say that she came of honest people. Always centred in his own alternating hopes and fears, and conscious of little in the lives of others, it seemed to him that a great difficulty had suddenly revealed itself to his apprehensions. At the same time, by a self-contradiction familiar to such natures as his, he felt himself more and more strongly drawn to the girl, and more and more strictly bound in honour to marry her. As he thought of this, his habitual contempt of the world and its opinion returned. What had the world done for him? And if he had felt no obligation to consult it in his poverty, why need he bend to any such slavery in the coming days of his splendour? He stopped suddenly at the corner of the street in which the Polish girl lived. She lodged, with a little sister who was still too young to work, in a room she hired of a respectable Bohemian shoemaker. The latter's wife was of the sour-good kind, whose chief talent lies in giving their kind actions a hard-hearted appearance.

"Vjera," said the Count, earnestly, "I have been talking a great deal about myself. You must forgive me, for the news I have received is so very important and makes such a sudden difference in my prospects. But you have not given me the answer I want to my question. Will you be my wife, Vjera, and come with me out of this wretched existence to share my happy life and to make it happier? Will you?"

His tone was so sincere and loving that it produced a little storm of evanescent happiness in the girl's heart, and the tears started to her eyes and stained her sallow, waxen cheeks.

"Ah, if it could only be true!" she exclaimed in a voice more than half full of hope, as she quickly brushed away the drops.

"But it is true, indeed it is," answered the Count. "Oh, Vjera, do you think I would deceive you? Do you think I could tell you a story in which there is no truth whatever? Do not think that of me, Vjera."

The tears broke out afresh, but from a different source. For some seconds she could not speak.

"Why do you cry so bitterly?" he asked, not understanding at all what was passing. "I swear to you it is all true—"

"It is not that—it is not that," cried Vjera. "I know—I know that you believe it—and I love you so very much—"

"But then, I do not understand," said the Count in a low voice that expressed his pitiful perplexity. "How can I not believe it, when it is all in the letters? And why should you not believe it, too? Besides, Vjera dear, it will all be quite clear to-morrow. Of course—well, I can understand that having known me poor so long, it must seem strange to you to think of me as very rich. But I shall not be another man, for that. I shall always be the same for you, Vjera, always the same."

"Yes, always the same," sighed the girl under her breath.

"Yes, and so, if you love me to-day, you will love me just as well to-morrow—to-morrow, the great day for me. What day will it be? Let me see—to-morrow is Wednesday."

"Wednesday, yes," repeated Vjera. "If only there were no to-morrow—" She checked herself. "I mean," she added, quickly, "if only it could be Thursday, without any day between."

"You are a strange girl, Vjera. I do not know what you are thinking of to-day. But to-morrow you will see. I think they will come for me in the morning. You shall see, you shall see."

Vjera began to move onward and the Count walked by her side, wondering at her manner and tormenting his brain in the vain effort to understand it. In front of her door he held out his hand.

"Promise me one thing," he said, as she laid her fingers in his and looked up at him. Her eyes were still full of tears.

"What is it?" she asked.

"Promise that you will be my wife, when you are convinced that all this good fortune is real. You do not believe in it, though I cannot tell why. I only ask that when you are obliged to believe in it, you will do as I ask."

Vjera hesitated, and as she stood still the hand he held trembled nervously.

"I promise," she said, at last, as though with a great effort. Then, all at once, she covered her eyes and leaned against the door-post. He laid his hand caressingly upon her shoulder.

"Is it so hard to say?" he asked, tenderly.

"Oh, but if it should ever be indeed true!" she moaned. "If it should—if it should!"

"What then? Shall we not be happy together? Will it not be even pleasant to remember these wretched years?"

"But if it should turn out so—oh, how can I ever be a fitting wife for you, how can I learn all that a great lady must think, and do, and say? I shall be unworthy of you—of your new friends, of your new world—but then, it cannot really happen. No—do not speak of it any more, it hurts me too much—good-night, good-night! Let us sleep and forget, and go back to our work in the morning, as though nothing had happened—in the morning, to-morrow. Will you? Then good-night."

"There will be no work to-morrow," he said, returning to his argument. But she broke away and fled from him and disappeared in the dark and narrow staircase. As he stood, he could hear her light tread on the creaking wood of the steps, fainter and fainter in the distance. Then he caught the feeble tinkle of a little bell, the opening and shutting of a door, and he was alone in the gloom of the evening.

For some minutes he stood still, as though listening for some faint echo from the direction in which Vjera had disappeared, then he slowly and thoughtfully walked away. He had forgotten to eat at dinner-time, and now he forgot that the hour of the second meal had come round. He walked on, not knowing and not caring whither he went, absorbed in the contemplation of the bright pictures which framed themselves in his brain, troubled only by his ever-recurring wonder at Vjera's behaviour.

Unconsciously, and from sheer force of habit, he threaded the streets in the direction of the tobacconist's shop where so much of his time was spent. If it be not true that the ghosts of the dead haunt places familiar to them in life, yet the superstition is founded upon the instincts of human nature. Men begin to haunt certain spots unconsciously while they are alive, especially those which they are obliged to visit every day and in which they are accustomed to sit, idle or at work, during the greater part of the week. The artist, when he wishes to be completely at rest, re-enters the studio he left but an hour earlier; the sailor hangs about the port when he is ashore, the shopman cannot resist the temptation to spend an hour among his wares on Sunday, the farmer is irresistibly drawn to the field to while away the time on holidays between dinner and supper. We all of us see more and understand better what we see, in those surroundings most familiar to us, and it is a general law that the average intelligence likes the best that which it understands with the least effort. The mechanical part of us, too, when free from any direct and especial impulse of the mind, does unknowingly what it has been in the habit of doing. Two-thirds of all the physical diseases in the world are caused by the disturbance of the mental habits and are vastly aggravated by the direction of the thoughts to the part afflicted. Idiots and madmen are often phenomenally healthy people, because there is in their case no unnatural effort of the mind to control and manage the body. The Count having bestowed no thought upon the direction of his walk, mechanically turned towards the scene of his daily labour.

Considering that he believed himself to have abandoned for ever the irksome employment of rolling tobacco in a piece of parchment in order to slip it into a piece of paper, it might have been supposed that he would be glad to look at anything rather than the glass door of the shop in which he had repeated that operation so many hundreds of thousands of times; or, at least, it might have been expected that on realising where he was he would be satisfied with a glance of recognition and would turn away.

But the Count's fate had ordained otherwise. When he reached the shop the lights were burning brightly in the show window and within. Through the glass door he could see that Fischelowitz was comfortably installed in a chair behind the counter, contentedly smoking one of his own best cigarettes, and smiling happily to himself through the fragrant cloud. If the tobacconist's wife had been present, the Count would have gone away without entering, for he did not like her, and had reason to suspect that she hated him, which was indeed the case. But Akulina was nowhere to be seen, the shop looked bright and cheerful, the Count was tired, he pushed the door and entered. Fischelowitz turned his head without modifying his smile, and seeing who his visitor was nodded familiarly. The Count raised his hat a little from his head and immediately replaced it.

"Good-evening, Herr Fischelowitz," he said, speaking, as usual, in German.

"Good-evening, Count," answered the tobacconist, cheerfully. "Sit down, and light a cigarette. What is the news?"

"Great news with me, for to-morrow," said the other, bending his head as he stooped over the nickel-plated lamp on the counter, in which a tiny flame burned for the convenience of customers. "To-morrow, at this time, I shall be on my way to Petersburg."

"Well, I hope so, for your sake," was the good-humoured reply. "But I am afraid it will always be to-morrow, Herr Graf."

The Count shook his head after staring for a few seconds at his employer, and then smoked quietly, as though he attached no weight to the remark. Fischelowitz looked curiously at him, and during a brief moment the smile faded from his face.

"You have not been long at supper," he remarked, after a pause. The observation was suggested by the condition of his own appetite.

"Supper?" repeated the Count, rather vaguely. "I believe I had forgotten all about it. I will go presently."

"The Count is reserving himself for to-morrow," said an ironical voice in the background. Akulina entered the shop from the workroom, a guttering candle in a battered candlestick in one hand, and a number of gaily coloured pasteboard boxes tucked under the other arm. "What is the use of eating to-day when there will be so many good things to-morrow?"

Neither Fischelowitz nor the Count vouchsafed any answer to this thrust. For the second time, since the Count had entered, however, the tobacconist wore an expression approaching to gravity. The Count himself kept his composure admirably, only glancing coldly at Akulina, and then looking at his cigarette. Akulina is a broad, fat woman, with a flattened Tartar face, small eyes, good but short teeth, full lips and a dark complexion. She reminds one of an over-fed tabby cat, of doubtful temper, and her voice seems to reach utterance after traversing some thick, soft medium, which lends it an odd sort of guttural richness. She moves quietly but heavily and has an Asiatic second sight in the matter of finance. In matters of thrift and foresight her husband places implicit confidence in her judgment. In matters of generosity and kindness implying the use of money, he never consults her.

"It is amazing to see how much people will believe," she said, putting out her candle and snuffing it with her thumb and forefinger. Then she began to arrange the boxes she had brought, setting them in order upon the shelves. Still neither of the men answered her. But she was not the woman to be reduced to silence by silence.

"I am always telling you that it is all rubbish," she continued, turning a broad expanse of alpaca-covered back upon her audience. "I am always telling you that you are no more a count than Fischelowitz is a grand duke, that the whole thing is a foolish imagination which you have stuck into your head, as one sticks tobacco into a paper shell. And it ought to be burned out of your head, or starved out, or knocked out, or something, for if it stays there it will addle your brains altogether. Why cannot you see that you are in the world just like other people, and give up all these ridiculous dreams and all this chatter about counts and princes and such like people, of whom you never spoke to one in your life, for all you may say?"

The Count glanced at the back of Akulina's head, which was decently covered by a flattened twist of very shining black hair, and then he looked at Fischelowitz as though to inquire whether the latter would suffer a gentleman to be thus insulted in his presence and on his premises. Fischelowitz seemed embarrassed, and coloured a little.

"You might choose your language a little more carefully, wife," he observed in a rather timid tone.

"And you might choose your friends with a better view to your own interests," she answered without hesitation. "If you allow this sort of thing to go on, and four children growing up, and you expecting to open another shop this summer—why, you had better turn count yourself," she concluded, triumphantly, and with that nice logical perception peculiar to her kind.

"If you mean to say that the Count's valuable help has not been to our advantage—" began Fischelowitz, making a desperate effort to give a more pleasant look to things.

"Oh, I know that," laughed Akulina, scornfully. "I know that the Count, as you call him, can make his two thousand a day as well as any one. I am not blind. And I know you, and I know that it is a sort of foolish pleasure to you to employ a count in the work and to pay your money to a count, though he does not earn it any better than any one else, nor any worse, to be just. And I know the Count, and I know his friends who borrow fifty marks of you and pay you back in stuffed dolls with tunes in them. I know you, Christian Gregorovitch"—at the thought of the lost money Akulina broke at last into her native language and gave the reins to her fury in good Russian—"yes, I know you, and him, and his friends and your friends, and I see the good yellow money flying out of the window like a flight of canary birds when the cage is opened, and I see you grinning like Player-Ape over the vile Vienna puppet, and winding up its abominable music as though you were turning the key upon your money in the safe instead of listening to the tune of its departure. And then because Akulina has the courage to tell you the truth, and to tell you that your fine Count is no count, and that his friends get from you ten times the money he earns, then you turn on me like a bear, ready to bite off my head, and you tell me to choose my language! Is there no shame in you, Christian Gregorovitch, or is there also no understanding? Am I the mother of your four children or not? I would like to ask. I suppose you cannot deny that, whatever else you deny which is true, and you tell me to choose my language! *Da,* I will choose my language, in truth! *Da,* I will choose out such a swarm of words as ought to sting your ears like hornets, if you had not such a leathery skin and such a soft brain inside it. But why should I? It is thrown away. There is no shame in you. You see nothing, you care for nothing, you hear no reason, you feel no argument. I will go home and make soup. I am better there than in the shop. Oh yes! it is always that. Akulina can make good things to eat, and good tea and good punch to drink, and Akulina is the Archangel Michael in the kitchen. But if Akulina says to you, 'Save a penny here, do not lend more than you have there,' Akulina is a fool and must be told to choose her language, lest it be too indelicate for the dandified ears of the high-born gentleman! I should not wonder if, by choosing her language carefully enough, Akulina ended by making the high-born gentleman understand something after all. His perception cannot possibly be so dull as yours, Christian Gregorovitch, my little husband."

Akulina paused for breath after her tremendous invective, which, indeed, was only intended by her for the preface of the real discourse, so fertile was her imagination and so thoroughly roused was her eloquence by the sense of injury received. While she was speaking, Fischelowitz, whose terror of his larger half was only relative, had calmly risen and had wound up the "Wiener Gigerl" to the extreme of the doll's powers, placing it on the counter before him and sitting down before it in anticipation of the amusement he expected to derive from its performance. In the short silence which ensued while Akulina was resting her lungs for a second and more deadly effort, the wretched little musical box made itself heard, clicking and scratching and grinding out a miserable little polka. At the sound, the sunny smile returned to the tobacconist's face. He knew that no earthly eloquence, no scathing wit, no brutal reply could possibly exasperate his wife as this must. He resented everything she had said, and in his vulgar way he was ashamed that she should have said it before the Count, and now he was glad that by the mere turning of a key he could answer her storm of words in a way to drive her to fury, while at the same time showing his own indifference. As for the Count himself, he had moved nearer to the door and was looking quietly out into the irregularly lighted street, smoking as though he had not heard a word of what had been said. As he stood, it was impossible for either of the others to see his face, and he betrayed no agitation by movement or gesture.

Akulina turned pale to the lips, as her husband had anticipated. It is probable that the most tragic event conceivable in her existence could not have affected her more powerfully than the twang of the musical box and the twisting and turning of the insolent little wooden head. She came round to the front of the counter with gleaming eyes and clenched fists.

"Stop that thing!" she cried, "Stop it, or it will drive me mad."

Fischelowitz still smiled, and the doll continued to turn round and round to the tune, while the Count looked out through the open door. Suddenly there was a quick shadow on the brightly lighted floor of the shop, followed instantly by a crash, and then with a miserable attempt to finish its tune the little instrument gave a resounding groan and was silent. Akulina had struck the Gigerl such a blow as had sent it flying, pedestal and all, past her husband's head into a dark corner behind the counter. Fischelowitz reddened with anger, and Akulina stood ready to take to flight, glad that the broad counter was between herself and her husband. Her fury had spent itself in one blow and she would have given anything to set the doll up in its place again unharmed. She realised at the same instant that she had probably destroyed any intrinsic value which the thing had possessed, and her face fell wofully. The Count turned slowly where he stood and looked at the couple.

"Are you going to fight each other?" he inquired in unusually bland tones.

At the sound of his voice the Russian woman's anger rose again, glad to find some new object upon which to expend itself and on which to exercise vengeance for the catastrophe its last expression had brought about. She turned savagely upon the Count and shook her plump brown fists in his face.

"It is all your fault!" she exclaimed. "What business have you to come between husband and wife with your friends and your cursed dolls, the fiend take them, and you! Is it for this that Christian Gregorovitch and I have lived together in harmony these ten years and more? Is it for this that we have lived without a word of anger—"

"What did you say?" asked Fischelowitz, with an angry laugh. But she did not heed him.

"Without a word of anger between us, these many years?" she continued. "Is it for this? To have our peace destroyed by a couple of Wiener Gigerls, a doll and a sham count? But it is over now! It is over, I tell you—go, get yourself out of the shop, out of my sight, into the street where you belong! For honest folks to be harbouring such a fellow as you are, and not you only, but your friends and your rag and your tag! Fie! If you stay here long we shall end in dust and feathers! But you shall not stay here, whatever that soft-brained husband of mine says. You shall go and never come back. Do you think that in all Munich there is no one else who will do the work for three marks a thousand? Bah! there are scores, and honest people, too, who call themselves by plain names and speak plainly! None of your counts and your grand dukes and your Lord-knows-whats! Go, you adventurer, you disturber of—why do you look at me like that? I have always known the truth about you, and I have never been able to bear the sight of you and never shall. You have deceived my husband, poor man, because he is not as clever as he is good-natured, but you never could deceive me, try as you would, and the Lord knows, you have tried often enough. Pah! You good-for-nothing!"

The poor Count had drawn back against the well-filled shop and had turned deadly pale as she heaped insult upon insult upon him in her incoherent and foul-mouthed anger. As soon as she paused, exhausted by the effort to find epithets to suit her hatred of him, he went up to the counter where Fischelowitz was sitting, very much disturbed at the course events were taking.

"My dear Count," began the latter, anxious to set matters right, "pray do not pay any attention—"

"I think I had better say good-bye," answered the Count in a low tone. "We part on good terms, though you might have said a word for me just now."

"He dare not!" cried Akulina.

"And as for the doll, if you will give it to me, I promise you that you shall have your fifty marks to-morrow."

"Oho! He knows where to get fifty marks, now!" exclaimed Akulina, viciously.

Fischelowitz picked up the puppet, which was broken in two in the waist, so that the upper half of the body hung down by the legs, in a limp fashion, held only by the little red coat. The tobacconist wrapped it up in a piece of newspaper without a word and handed it to the Count. He felt perhaps that the only atonement he could offer for his wife's brutal conduct was to accede to the request.

"Thank you," said the Count, taking the thing. "On the word of a gentleman you shall have the money before to-morrow night."

"A good riddance of both of them," snarled Akulina, as the Count lifted his hat and then, his head bent more than was his wont, passed out of the shop with the remains of the poor Gigerl under his arm.

CHAPTER IV

The Count had no precise object in view when he hurriedly left the shop with the parcel containing the broken doll. What he most desired for the moment was to withdraw himself from the storm of Akulina's abuse, seeing that he had no means of checking the torrent, nor of exacting satisfaction for the insults received. However he might have acted had the aggressor been a man, he was powerless when attacked by a woman, and he was aware that he had followed the only course which had in it anything of dignity and self-respect. To stand and bandy words and epithets of abuse would have been worse than useless, to treat the tobacconist like a gentleman and to hold him responsible for his wife's language would have been more than absurd. So the Count took the remains of the puppet and went on his way.

He was not, however, so superior to good and bad treatment as not to feel deeply wounded and thoroughly roused to anger. Perhaps, if he had been already in possession of the fortune and dignity which he expected on the morrow, he might have smiled contemptuously at the virago's noisy wrath, feeling nothing and caring even less what she felt towards him. But he had too long been poor and wretched to bear with equanimity any reference to his wretchedness or his poverty, and he was too painfully conscious of the weight of outward circumstances in determining men's judgments of their fellows not to be stung by the words that had been so angrily applied to him. Moreover, and worst of all, there was the fact that Fischelowitz had really lent the money to a poor countryman who had previously made the acquaintance of the Count, and had by that means induced the tobacconist to help him. It was true, indeed, that the poor Count had himself lent the fellow all he had in his pocket, which meant all that he had in the world, and had been half starved in consequence during a whole week. The man was an idle vagabond of the worst type, with a pitiful tale of woe well worded and logically put together, out of which he made a good livelihood. Nature, as though to favour his designs, had given him a face which excited sympathy, and he had the wit to cover his eyes, his own tell-tale feature, with coloured glasses. He had cheated several scores of persons in the Slav colony of Munich, and had then gone in search of other pastures. How he had obtained possession of the Wiener Gigerl was a mystery as yet unsolved. It had certainly seemed odd in the tobacconist's opinion that a man of such outward appearance should have received such an extremely improbable Christmas present, for such the adventurer declared the doll to be, from a rich aunt in Warsaw, who refused to give him a penny of ready money and had caused him to be turned from her doors by her servants when he had last visited her, on the ground that he had joined the Russian Orthodox Church without her consent. The facetious young villain had indeed declared that she had sent him the puppet as a piece of scathing irony, illustrative of his character as she conceived it. But though such an illustration would have been apt beyond question, yet it seemed improbable that the aunt would have chosen such a means of impressing it upon her nephew's mind. Fischelowitz, however, asked no questions, and took the Gigerl as payment of the debt. The thing amused him, and it diverted him to construct an imaginary chain of circumstances to explain how the man in the coloured glasses had got possession of it. It was of course wholly inconceivable that even the most accomplished shop-lifter should have carried off an object of such inconvenient proportions from the midst of its fellows and under the very eyes of the vendor. If he had supposed a theft possible, Fischelowitz would never have allowed the doll to remain on his premises a single day. He was too kind-hearted, also, to blame the Count, as his wife did, for having been the promoter of the loan, for he readily admitted that he would have lent as much, had he made the vagabond's acquaintance under any other circumstances.

But the Count, since Akulina had expressed herself with so much force and precision, could not look upon the affair in the same light. However Fischelowitz regarded it, Akulina had made it clear that the Count ought to be held responsible for the loss, and it was not in the nature of such a man, no matter how wretched his own estate, to submit to the imputation of being concerned in borrowing money which was never to be repaid. His natural impulse had been to promise repayment instantly, and as he was expecting to be turned into a rich man on the morrow the engagement seemed an easy one to keep. It would be more difficult to explain why he wanted to take away the broken puppet with him. Possibly he felt that in removing it from the shop, he was taking with it even the memory of the transaction of which the blame had been so bitterly thrown on him; or, possibly, he was really attached to the toy for its associations, or, lastly, he may have felt impelled to save it from Akulina's destroying wrath, so far as it yet could be said to be saved.

As has been said, he had not dined on that day, and he would very probably have forgotten to eat, even after being reminded of the meal by the tobacconist, had he not passed, on his way homeward, the obscure restaurant in which he and the other men who worked for Fischelowitz were accustomed to get their food and drink. This fifth-rate eating-house rejoiced in the attractive name of the "Green Wreath," a designation painted in large dusty green Gothic letters upon the grey walls of the dilapidated house in which it was situated. There are not to be found in respectable Munich those dens of filth and drunkenness which belong to greater cities whose vices are in proportion greater also. In Munich the strength of fiery spirits is drowned in oceans of mild beer, a liquid of which the head will stand more than the waistband and which, instead of exciting to crime, predisposes the consumer to peaceful and lengthened sleep. The worst that can be said of the poorer public-houses in Munich, is that they are frequented by the poorer people, and that as the customers bring less money than elsewhere, there is less drinking in proportion, and a greater demand for large quantities of very filling food at very low rates. As a general rule, such places are clean and decently kept, and the sight of a drunken man in the public room would excite very considerable astonishment, besides entailing upon the culprit a summary expulsion into the street and a rather forcible injunction not to repeat the offence.

The four windows of the establishment which opened upon the narrow street were open, for the weather had become sultry even out of doors, and the guests wanted fresh air. At one of these windows the Count saw the heads of Dumnoff and Schmidt. With the instinct of the poor man, the Count felt in his pocket to see whether he had any money, and was somewhat disturbed to find but a solitary piece of silver, feebly supported on either side by a couple of one-penny pieces. He had forgotten that he had refused to accept his pay for the day's work, and it required an effort of memory to account for the low state of his funds. But what he had with him was sufficient for his wants, and settling his parcel under his arm he ascended the three or four steps which gave access to the inn, and entered the public room. Besides the Russian and the Cossack, there were three public porters seated at the next table, dressed in their blue blouses, their red cloth caps hanging on the pegs over their heads, all silent and similarly engaged. Each had before him a piece of that national cheese of which the smell may almost be heard, each had lately received a thick, irregularly-shaped hunch of dark bread, and they had one pot of beer and one salt-cellar amongst them. They all had honest German faces, honest blue eyes, horny hands and round shoulders. Another table, in a far corner, was occupied by a poorly-dressed old woman in black, dusty and evidently tired. A covered basket stood on a chair at her elbow, she was eating an unwholesome-looking "knödel" or boiled potato ball, and half a pint of beer stood before her still untouched. As for the Cossack and Dumnoff, they had finished their meal. The former was smoking a cigarette through a mouth-piece made by boring out the well-dried leg-bone of a chicken and was drinking nothing. Dumnoff had before him a small glass of the common whisky known as "corn-brandy" and was trying to give it a flavour resembling the vodka of his native land by stirring pepper into it with the blade of an old pocket-knife. Both looked up, without betraying any surprise, as the Count entered and sat himself down at the end of their oblong table, facing the open window and with his back to the room. A word of greeting passed on each side and the two relapsed into silence, while the Count ordered a sausage "with horse-radish" of the sour-sweet maiden of five-and-thirty who waited on the guests. The Cossack, always observant of such things, looked at the oddly-shaped package which the Count had brought with him, trying to divine its contents and signally failing in the attempt. Dumnoff, who did not like the Count's gentlemanlike manners and fine speech, sullenly stirred the fiery mixture he was concocting. The colour on his prominent cheek-bones was a little brighter than before supper, but otherwise it was impossible to say that he was the worse for the half-pint of spirits he had certainly absorbed since leaving his work. The man's strong peasant nature was proof against far greater excesses than his purse could afford.

"What is the news?" inquired Johann Schmidt, still eyeing the bundle curiously, and doubtless hoping that the Count would soon inform him of the contents. But the latter saw the look and glanced suspiciously at the questioner.

"No news, that I know of," he answered. "Except for me," he added, after a pause, and looking dreamily out of the window at a street lamp that was burning opposite. "To-morrow, at this time, I shall be off."

"And where are you going?" asked the Cossack, good-humouredly. "Are you going for long, if I may ask?"

"Yes—yes. I shall never come back to Munich." He had been speaking in German, but noticing that the other guests in the room were silent, and thinking that they might listen, he broke off into Russian. "I shall go home, at last," he said, his face brightening perceptibly as his visions of wealth again rose before his eyes. "I shall go home and rest myself for a long time in the country, and then, next winter, perhaps, I will go to Petersburg."

"Well, well, I wish you a pleasant journey," said Schmidt. "So there is to be no mistake about the fortune this time?"

"This time?" repeated the Count, as though not understanding. "Why do you say this time?"

"Because you have so often expected it before," returned the Cossack bluntly, but without malice.

"I do not remember ever saying so," said the other, evidently searching among his recollections.

"Every Tuesday," growled Dumnoff, sipping his peppery liquor. "Every Tuesday since I can remember."

"I think you must be mistaken," said the Count, politely.

Dumnoff grunted something quite incomprehensible, and which might have been taken for the clearing of his huge throat after the inflaming draught. The Cossack was silent, and his bright eyes looked pityingly at his companion.

"And you have begun to put together your parcels for the journey, I see," he observed after a time, when the Count had got his morsel of food and was beginning to eat it. His curiosity gave him no rest.

"Yes," answered the Count, mysteriously. "That is something which I shall probably take with me, as a remembrance of Munich."

"I should not have thought that you needed anything more than a cigarette to remind you of the place," remarked Dumnoff.

The Count smiled faintly, for, considering Dumnoff's natural dulness, the remark had a savour of wit in it.

"That is true," he said. "But there are other things which could remind me even more forcibly of my exile."

"Well, what is it? Tell us!" cried Dumnoff, impatiently enough, but somewhat softened by the Count's appreciation of his humour. At the same time he put out his broad red hand in the direction of the parcel as though he would see for himself.

"Let it be!" said Schmidt sharply, and Dumnoff withdrew his hand again. He had fallen into the habit of always doing what the Cossack told him to do, obeying mutely, like a well-trained dog, though he obeyed no one else. The descendant of freemen instinctively lorded it over the descendant of the serf, and the latter as instinctively submitted.

The Count's temper, however, was singularly changeable on this day, for he did not seem to resent Dumnoff's meditated attack upon the package, as he would certainly have done under ordinary circumstances.

"If you are so very curious to know what it is, I will tell you," he said. "You know the Wiener Gigerl?"

"Of course," answered both men together.

"Well, that is it, in that parcel."

"The Gigerl!" exclaimed the Cossack. Dumnoff only opened his small eyes in stupid amazement. Both knew something of the circumstances under which Fischelowitz had come into possession of the doll, and both knew what store the tobacconist set by it.

"Then you have paid the fifty marks?" asked Schmidt, whose curiosity was roused instead of satisfied.

"No. I shall pay the money to-morrow. I have promised to do so. As it chances, it will be convenient." The Count smiled to himself in a meaning way, as though already enjoying the triumph of laying the gold pieces upon the counter under Akulina's flat nose.

"And yet Fischelowitz has already given it to you! He must be very sure of you—" With his usual lack of tact, Schmidt had gone further than he meant to do, but the transaction savoured of the marvellous.

"To be strictly truthful," said the Count, who had a Quixotic fear of misleading in the smallest degree any one to whom he was speaking, "to be exactly honest, there is a circumstance which makes it less remarkable that Fischelowitz should have given me the doll at once."

"Of course, of course!" exclaimed the Cossack, anxious to appear credulous out of kindness. "Fischelowitz knows as well as you do yourself how safe you are to get the money to-morrow."

"Naturally," replied the Count, with great calmness. "But besides that, the Gigerl is broken—badly broken in the middle, and the musical box is spoiled too."

"Fischelowitz must have been very angry," observed Dumnoff.

"Not at all. It was his wife. Akulina knocked it from the counter into the farthest corner of the shop."

"Tell us all about it," said Schmidt, more interested than ever.

"Ah, that—that is quite another matter," answered the Count, reddening perceptibly as he remembered Akulina's furious abuse.

"If you do not, I have no doubt that she will," said Dumnoff, taking another sip. "She always gives the news of you, before you come in the morning, before we have made our first hundred."

The Count grew redder still, the angry colour mantling in his lean cheeks. He hesitated a moment, and then made up his mind.

"If that is likely to happen," he cried, "I had better tell you the truth myself, instead of giving her an opportunity of distorting it."

"Much better," said the Cossack, eagerly. "One can believe you better than her."

"That is true, at all events," chimed in Dumnoff, who was only brutal and never malicious.

"Well, it happened in this way. Fischelowitz and I were talking of to-morrow, I think, when she came in from the back shop, having overheard something we had been saying. Of course she immediately took advantage of my presence to exercise her wit upon me, a proceeding to which I have grown accustomed, seeing that she is only a woman. Then Fischelowitz told her to choose her language, and that started her afresh. It was rather a fine specimen of chosen language that she gave us, for she has a good command of our beautiful mother-tongue. She found very strong words, and she said among other things that it was my fault that her husband had got a Wiener Gigerl for fifty marks of good money. And then Fischelowitz, in his easy way and while she was talking, wound the doll up and set it before him on the counter and smiled at it. But she went on, worse than before, and called me everything under the sun. Of course I could do nothing but wait until she had finished, for I could not beat her, and I would not let her think that she could drive me away by mere talk, bad as it was."

"What did she call you?" asked Dumnoff, with a grin.

"She called me a good-for-nothing," said the Count, reddening with anger again, so that the veins stood out on his throat above his collar. "And she called me, I think, an adventurer."

"Is that all?" laughed Dumnoff. "I have been called by worse names than that in my time!"

"I have not," answered the Count, with sudden coolness. "However, between me and Fischelowitz and the Gigerl, she grew so angry that she struck the only one of us three against whom she dared lift hand. That member of the company chanced to be the unfortunate doll. And then I promised that to-morrow I would pay the money, and I made Fischelowitz give it to me in a piece of newspaper, and there it is."

"What a terrible smash there must have been in the shop!" said Dumnoff. "I would like to have seen the lady's face."

In their Russian speech, the difference between the original social standing of the three men who now worked as equals, was well defined by their way of speaking of Fischelowitz's wife. To Dumnoff, mujik by origin and by nature, she was "barina," the town "lady," to the Cossack she was "chosjaika," the "mistress," the wife of the "patron"—to the Count she was Akulina, and when he addressed her he called her Akulina Feodorovna, adding the derivative of her father's name in accordance with the universal Russian custom.

"Let us see the doll," said Schmidt, still curious. The Count, whose eating had been interrupted by the telling of his story, pushed the parcel towards the Cossack with one hand, while using his fork with the other.

Johann Schmidt carefully unwrapped the newspaper and exposed the unfortunate Gigerl to view. Then with both hands he set it up before him, raising the limp figure from the waist, and trying to put it into position, until it almost recovered something of its old look of insolence, though the eye-glass was broken and the little white hat sadly battered. The three men contemplated it in silence, and the other guests turned curious glances towards it. Dumnoff, as usual, laughed hoarsely.

"Rather the worse for wear," he observed.

"Kreuzmillionendonnerwetter! That is my Gigerl!" roared a deep German voice across the room.

The three Russians started and looked round quickly. One of the porters, a burly man with an angry scowl on his honest face, was already on his legs and was striding towards the table.

"That is my Gigerl!" he repeated, laying one heavy hand upon the board, and thrusting the forefinger of the other under the doll's nose.

Dumnoff stared at him with an expression which showed that he did not in the least understand what was happening. Johann Schmidt's keen black eyes looked wonderingly from the porter to the Count, while the latter leaned back in his chair, contemplating the angry man with a calm surprise which proved how little faith he placed in the assertion of possession.

"You are under a mistake," he said, with great politeness. "This doll is the property of Herr Fischelowitz, the well-known tobacconist, and has stood in the window of his shop nearly four months. These gentlemen"—he waved his hand towards his two companions—"are well aware of the fact and can vouch—"

"That is all the same to me," interrupted the porter. "This is the Gigerl which was stolen from me on New Year's eve—"

"I repeat," said the Count, with dignity, "that you are altogether mistaken. I will trouble you to leave us in peace and to make no more disturbance, where you are evidently in error."

His coolness exasperated the porter, who seemed very sure of what he asserted.

"That is what we shall see," he retorted in a menacing tone. "Meanwhile it does not occur to me to leave you in peace and to make no more trouble. I tell you that this Gigerl was stolen from me on New Year's eve. I know it well enough, for I had to pay for it."

"How can you prove that this is the one?" inquired the Cossack, who was beginning to lose his temper.

"You have nothing to say about it," said the porter, sharply. "I have to do with this man"—he pointed down at the Count—"who has brought the doll here, and pretends to know where it comes from."

"Kerl!" exclaimed the Count, angrily. "Fellow! I am not accustomed to being called 'man,' or to having my word doubted. You had better be civil."

"Then it is high time that you grew used to it," returned the porter, growing more and more excited. "The police do not overwhelm fellows of your kind with politeness."

"Fellows?" cried the Count, losing his self-control altogether at being called by the name he had just applied to the porter. Without a moment's hesitation, he sprang from his chair, upsetting it behind him, and took the burly German by the throat.

"Call a policeman, Anton!" shouted the latter to one of his companions, as he closed with his antagonist.

The two other porters had risen from their places as soon as the Count had laid his hands on their friend, and the one who answered to the name of Anton promptly trotted towards the door, his heavy tread making the whole room shake as he ran. The other came up quickly and attacked the Count from behind, when Dumnoff, aroused at last to the pleasant consciousness that a real fight was going on, brought down his clenched fist with such earnestness of purpose on the top of the second porter's crown that the latter reeled backwards and fell across the Count's chair in an attitude rendered highly uncomfortable by the fact that the said chair had been turned upside down at the beginning of the contest. Having satisfied himself that the blow had taken effect, Dumnoff proceeded to the other side of the field of battle, avoiding the quickly moving bodies of the Count and the porter as they wrestled with each other, and the mujik prepared to deal another sledge-hammer blow, in all respects comparable with the first. A pleasant smile beamed and spread over his broad, bony face as he lifted his fist, and it is comparatively certain that he would have put an effectual end to the struggle, had not Schmidt interfered with the execution of his amiable intentions by catching his arm in mid-air. Even the Cossack's wiry strength could not arrest the descent of the tremendous fist, but he succeeded at least in diverting it from its aim, so that it took effect in the middle of the porter's back, knocking most of the wind out of the man's body and causing a diversion favourable to the Count's security. Schmidt sprang in and separated the combatants.

"There has been enough dancing already," he said, coolly, as he faced the porter, who was gasping for breath. "But if you have not danced enough, I shall be happy to take a turn with you round the room."

The poor Count would, indeed, have been no match for his adversary without the assistance of his friends. He possessed that sort of courage which, when stung into activity by an insult, takes no account whatever of the consequences, and his thin frame was animated by very excitable nerves. But an exceedingly lean diet, and the habit of sitting during many hours in a close atmosphere, rolling tobacco with his fingers, did not constitute such a physical training as to make him a match for a rough fellow whose occupation consisted in tramping long distances and up and down long flights of stairs from morning till night, loaded with more or less heavy burdens. He was now very pale and his heart beat painfully as he endeavoured instinctively to smooth his long frock-coat, from which a button had been torn out by the roots in a very apparent place, and to settle his starched collar, which at the best of times owed its stability to the secret virtues of a pin, and which at present had made a quarter of a revolution upon itself, so that the stiffly-starched corners, the Count's chief coquetry and pride, had established themselves in an unseemly manner immediately below the left ear.

Meanwhile, the little restaurant was in an uproar. The host, a thin, pale man in an apron and a shabby embroidered cap, had suddenly appeared from the depths of the taproom, accompanied by his wife, a monstrous, red-faced creature clothed in a grey flannel frock. The porter whom Dumnoff had felled, and who was not altogether stunned, was kicking violently in the attempt to gain his feet among the fallen chairs, a dozen people had come in from the street at the noise of the fight and stood near the door, phlegmatically watching the proceedings, and the poor old woman from the country, who had been supping in the corner, had got her basket on her knees, holding its handle tightly in one hand and with the other grasping her half-finished glass of beer, in terror lest some accident should cause the precious liquid to be spilled, but not calm enough to put it in a place of safety by the simple process of swallowing.

"They are foreigners," remarked some one in the crowd at the door.

"They are probably Bohemian journeymen," said a tinman who stood in front of the others. "It serves them right for interfering with an honest porter." The Bohemian journeymen are detested in Munich on account of their willingness to work for low prices, which perhaps accounted for the tinman's readiness to consider the strangers as worsted in the contest.

"We Germans fear God, and nothing else in the world," observed a mealy-faced shoemaker, quoting Prince Bismarck's famous speech.

The man who had wrestled with the Count seemed to have resigned himself to the course of awaiting the police, and leaned back against the table behind him, with folded arms, glaring at the Cossack, while the Count was vainly attempting to recover possession of the pin which had fastened his collar, and which he evidently suspected of having slipped down his back, with the total depravity peculiar to all inanimate things when they are most needed. But the second porter, having broken the chair, upset a table covered with unused saucers for beer glasses, and otherwise materially contributing to swell the din and increase the already considerable havoc, had regained his feet and lost no time in making for Dumnoff. The Russian, enchanted at the prospect of a renewal of hostilities so unfortunately interrupted, met the newcomer half-way, and, each embracing the other with cheerful alacrity, the two heavy men began to stamp and turn round and round with each other like a couple of particularly awkward bears attempting to waltz together. They were very evenly matched for a wrestling bout, for although the German was by a couple of inches the taller of the two, the Russian had the advantage in breadth of shoulder and length of arm, as well as in the enormous strength of his back. The Cossack, having assured himself that there was to be fair-play, watched the proceedings with evident interest, while the pale-faced host shambled round and round the room, imploring the combatants to respect the reputation of his house and to desist, while keeping himself at a safe distance from possible collision with the bodies of the two, as they staggered and strained, and reeled and whirled about.

The Count at last abandoned the search of the lost pin, and having pulled the front of his collar into a more normal position trusted to luck to keep it there. The table at which the three had originally sat had miraculously escaped upsetting, and on it lay the poor Gigerl, stretched at full length on its back, calm and smiling in the midst of the noise and confusion, like the corpse at an Irish wake after the whisky has begun to take effect.

The Count now thought it necessary to justify the unfortunate situation in which he found himself, in the judgment of the spectators.

"Gentlemen," he began, very earnestly and with a dignified gesture, "I feel it necessary to explain the truth of this—" But he was interrupted by the arrival of a policeman, who pushed his way through the crowd.

CHAPTER V

"What is this row?" inquired the policeman in his official voice, as he marched into the room.

The man who was wrestling with Dumnoff was a German and a soldier. At the authoritative words he relaxed his hold and made an effort to free himself, a movement of which the Russian instantly took advantage by throwing his adversary heavily, upsetting another table and thereby bringing the confusion to its crisis. How far he would have gone if he had been left to himself is uncertain, for the sudden appearance of two more men in green coats, helmets and gold collars so emboldened the spectators of the fight that they advanced in a body just as Dumnoff threw himself upon the first policeman. The Russian's red face was wet with perspiration, his small eyes were gleaming ferociously and his thick hair hung in tangled locks over his forehead, producing with his fair beard the appearance of a wild animal's mane. But for the timely assistance of his colleagues, the representatives of the law, and, most likely the majority of the spectators would have found themselves in the street in an exceedingly short space of time. But Dumnoff yielded to the inevitable; a couple of well-planted blows delivered by the rescuing party on the sides of his thick skull made him shake his head as a cat does when its nose is sprinkled with water, and the mujik reluctantly relinquished the struggle. At the same time the porter who had claimed the doll came forward and touched his bare head with a military salute.

"What is your name?" asked the first policeman, anxious to get to business.

"Jacob Goggelmann, Dienstmann number 87, formerly private in the Fourth Artillery, lately messenger in the Thüringer Doll Manufactory."

"Very good," said the policeman, anxious to take the side of his countryman from the first, and certainly justified in doing so by the circumstances. "And what is your complaint?"

"That doll, there, on the table," said the porter, "was stolen from me on New Year's eve, and now that man"—he pointed to the Count, who stood stiffly looking on—"that man has got possession of it."

"And who stole it from you?" inquired the policeman with that acuteness in the art of cross-examination for which the police are in all countries so justly famous.

"Ja, Herr Wachtmeister, if I had known that—" suggested the porter.

"Of course, of course," interrupted the other. "That man stole the doll from you, you say?"

"Somebody stole it with my basket, as I stopped to drink a measure in the yard of the Hofbräuhaus, and I had to pay for it out of my caution money, and I lost my place into the bargain, and there lies the accursed thing."

The policeman, apparently quite satisfied with the porter's story, turned upon the Count with a blustering and overbearing manner.

"Now, then," he said, roughly, "give an account of yourself. Who are you and what are you doing here? But that is a foolish question; I know already that you are a Bohemian and a journeyman tinker."

"A Bohemian? And a journeyman tinker?" repeated the Count, almost speechless with anger for a moment. "I am neither," he added, endeavouring to control himself, and settling his refractory collar with one hand. "I am a Russian gentleman."

"A gentleman—and a Russian," said the policeman, slowly, as though putting no faith in the first statement and very little in the second. "I think I can provide you with a lodging for the night," he added, facetiously.

"Slip past me, jump out of the window and run!" whispered the Cossack in the Count's ear, in Russian.

"What are you saying in your infernal language?" asked the official.

"My friend advised me to run away," said the Count, coolly sitting down, as though he were master of the situation. "Unfortunately for me, I was not taught to use my legs in that way when I was a boy."

"I was," said the Cossack. "Good-evening, Master Policeman." He took his hat from the peg on the wall where it had hung undisturbed throughout the confusion, and bowing gravely to the man in uniform made as though he would go out of the room.

"So, so, not quite so fast, my friend," said the policeman, putting himself in the way. "Heigh! heigh! Stop him! Don't let him go," he bawled, a second later.

Schmidt had paused a minute, watching his opportunity, then, taking a quick step backwards, he had vaulted through the open window with the agility of a cat, and was flying down the empty street at the speed only attainable by that deceptive domestic animal when pressed for time and anxious for its own safety.

"Sobáka!" growled Domnoff, disgusted at his companion's defection.

"Either talk in a language that human beings can understand, or do not talk at all," said one of the two men who guarded him.

Seeing that pursuit was useless, the spokesman of the police turned to the Count, twice as blustering and terrible as before.

"This settles the question," he said. "To the police station you go, you and your bear-man of an accomplice. Potzbombardendonnerwetter! You Sappermentskerls! I will teach you to resist the police, to steal dolls and to jump out of windows! Now then, right about face—march!"

The Count did not stir from his chair. Dumnoff looked at him as though to ask instructions of a superior.

"If you can manage one of them, I can take these two," he said in Russian. Suiting the action to the word, he suddenly bent down, slipped his arms round the legs of the two policemen, hurled them simultaneously head over heels and then charged the crowd, head downwards, upsetting every one who came in his way, and bursting into the street by sheer superior weight and impetus. An instant later, his shock head appeared at the window through which the Cossack had escaped.

"Come along!" he shouted to the Count, in his own language. "I have locked the street door and they cannot get out. Jump through the window."

"Go, my friend," answered the Count, calmly. "I will not run away."

"You had much better come," insisted Dumnoff, apparently indifferent to the noise of the crowd as it tried to force open the closed door, and shaking off two or three men who had made their way out into the street with him. He held the key in one hand, and his assailants had small chance of getting it away.

"You will not come?" he repeated. But the Count shook his head, within the room.

"Then I will not run away either," said Dumnoff, the good side of his dull nature showing itself at last. With the utmost indifference to consequences he returned to the door, unlocked it, and strode through the midst of the people, who made way readily enough before him, after their late painful experience of his manner of making way for himself.

"I have changed my mind," he said, in German, quietly placing himself between his late keepers, who were alternately rubbing themselves and brushing the dust off each other's clothes after their tumble.

In the astonished silence which succeeded Dumnoff's return, the Count's voice was heard again.

"I am both anxious and ready to explain everything, if you will do me the civility to listen," he said. "The doll is the property of Herr Fischelowitz, the well-known tobacconist—"

"We shall see presently what you have to say for yourself," interrupted the policeman. "We have had enough of these devilish fellows. Come, put them in handcuffs and off with them. And you three gentlemen," he added, turning to the three porters, "will have the goodness to accompany us to the station, in order to give your evidence."

"But my furniture and my beer saucers!" exclaimed the pallid host, suddenly remembering his losses. "Who is to pay for them?"

The Count answered the question for him.

"You, Master Host, who know us and have had our regular custom for years, but who have not dared to say a word in our defence throughout this disgraceful affair, you, I say, deserve to lose all that you have lost. Nevertheless, I can assure you that I will myself pay for what has been broken."

The host was not much consoled by this magnanimous promise, which was received with jeers by the crowd. There was no time, however, to discuss the question. Dumnoff had quietly submitted his two huge fists to the handcuffs and a second pair was produced, to fit the Count. At this indignity he drew himself up proudly.

"Have I resisted the authority, or attempted to run away?" he inquired with flashing eyes.

The policeman had nothing to say to this very just question.

"Then I advise you to consider what you are doing. In spite of my appearance, which, I admit, is at present somewhat disorderly, I am a Russian nobleman, as you will discover so soon as I am submitted to a properly conducted examination in the presence of your officers. I have not the least intention of running away, and if this doll was stolen, I was not connected in any way with the theft. Since I respect the authorities, I insist upon being respected by them, and if I am treated in a degrading manner in spite of my protests, there are those in Munich who will bring the case to proper notice in my own country. I am ready to accompany you quietly wherever you choose to show me the way."

Something in his manner impressed the officials with the possible truth of his words. They looked at each other and nodded.

"Very well," said the one who was conducting the arrest.

"Moreover," said the Count, "I crave permission to carry myself the object of contention, until the other claimant has established his right of possession."

So saying the Count took the broken Gigerl from the table where it lay, and carrying it upon his hands before him, like a baby, he solemnly walked in the direction of the door, thus heading the procession, which was accompanied into the street by the idlers who had collected inside.

"God be thanked," said the old woman in the corner devoutly, "I have yet my beer!"

"And to think that only one of them has paid for his supper," moaned the pale-faced innkeeper, sitting down upon a chair and contemplating the wreck of his belongings with a haggard eye. The "Gigerl-night" was remembered for many a long year in the "Green Wreath Inn."

At the police station the arresting party told their own story in their own way, very much to the disadvantage of the Russians and very much in favour of the porters and of the officials themselves. The latter, indeed, enlarged so much upon the atrocities perpetrated by Dumnoff as to weary the superior officer. The Cossack having escaped, the policemen did not mention him. The officer glanced at Dumnoff.

"Your name?" he inquired.

"Victor Ivanowitch Dumnoff."

"Occupation?"

"Cigarette-maker in the manufactory of Christian Fischelowitz."

"Lock him up," said the officer. "Resisting the police in the execution of an arrest," he added, speaking to the scribe at his elbow.

"Your name?" continued he, addressing the Count. "Boris Michaelovitch, Count Skariatine."

"Count?" repeated the officer. "We shall see. Occupation?"

"I have been occupied in the manufacture of cigarettes," answered the Count. "But as I was only engaged in this during a period of temporary embarrassment from which I shall be relieved to-morrow, I may be described as having no particular occupation."

The officer stared incredulously for a moment and then nodded to the scribe in token that he was to write down what was said.

"Charged with having stolen a doll, is that it?" He turned to the policeman in charge.

"Jawohl, Herr Hauptmann."

"May it please you, Herr Hauptmann, I did not say that," put in the porter, coming forward.

"Who are you?"

"The man from whom the doll was stolen. Jacob Goggelmann, Dienstmann number 87, formerly private in the Fourth Artillery, lately messenger in the Thüringer Doll Manufactory."

"When was the doll stolen?"

"Last New Year's eve," answered the porter.

"And you have not seen it until to-day?"

"No, Herr Hauptmann."

"Then how do you know it is the same one? I suppose it is not the only doll of its kind in Munich."

"I am sure of it. I was a messenger in the shop, Herr Hauptmann, and I knew everything there, just as though I had been one of the young ladies who serve the customers. Besides, you will find my name written in pencil under the pedestal."

"That is another matter," said the officer, taking the Gigerl and holding it upside down to the gaslight. The reversing of the thing's natural position produced some mysterious effect upon the musical box, and the tune which had been so rudely interrupted by Akulina's well-aimed blow, suddenly began again from the point at which it had stopped, continuing for a few bars and then coming to an end with a sharp twang and a little click. The policemen tittered audibly, and even the captain smiled faintly in his big yellow beard. Then he knit his brows as he deciphered something which was written on the pinewood under the base.

"You should have said so at once," he observed. "Your name is there, as you assert."

"It was written to show that I was to take it. I had it in a basket with other things. I put it down a moment in the yard of the Hofbräuhaus, and when I came back the basket was gone."

"And what do you know about it?" The question was addressed to the Count.

"Seeing that the porter is evidently right," said the Count, covering with his hat the point from which the button had been torn, and holding the other hand rather nervously to his throat, as though trying to keep himself from falling to pieces, "I have nothing more to say. I will not be accused of inculpating any one in this disastrous affair. I will only say that the doll has stood since early in the year in the show window of Christian Fischelowitz, the tobacconist, who certainly had no knowledge of the way in which it was obtained by the person who brought it to him."

"He is an extremely respectable person," observed the officer. "If you can prove what you say, I will not detain you further. Have you any witness here?"

"There is Herr Dumnoff," said the Count. The officer smiled and perpetrated an official jest.

"Herr Dumnoff has given evidence of great strength, but owing to his peculiar situation at the present time, I cannot trust to the strength of his evidence."

The policemen laughed respectfully.

"Have you no one else?" asked the officer.

"Herr Fischelowitz will willingly vouch for what I say."

"At this hour, Herr Fischelowitz is doubtless asleep, and would certainly be justified in refusing to come here out of mere complaisance. I am afraid, Count Skariatine, that I must have the honour of being your host until morning."

"It is impossible to describe our relative positions with greater courtesy," answered the Count, gravely, and not taking the least notice of the officer's ironical tone. The latter looked at the speaker curiously and then suddenly changed his manner. He was convinced that he was speaking with a gentleman.

"I regret that I am obliged to put you to such inconvenience," he said, politely. "Treat the gentleman with every consideration," he added, addressing the policemen in a tone of authority, "and let me have no complaints of unnecessary rudeness either."

"I thank you, Herr Hauptmann," said the Count, simply.

Thus was the Count deprived of his liberty on the very eve of his return to all the brilliant advantages of wealth and social station. It was certainly a most unfortunate train of circumstances which had led him by such quick stages from his parting with Vjera to the wooden bench and the board pillow of the police-station. It looked as though the Gigerl were possessed of an evil spirit determined to work out the Count's destruction, as though the wretched adventurer who had first stolen it and palmed it off upon Fischelowitz had laid a curse upon it, whereby it was destined to breed dissension and strife wherever it remained and to the direct injury of whomsoever chanced to possess it for the time being. It had been the cause of serious disaster to the porter in the first instance, it had next represented to Fischelowitz a dead loss in money of fifty marks, it had become a thorn in the side to Akulina, it had led to one of the most violent quarrels she had ever engaged in with her husband, its limp and broken form had cost much broken crockery and some broken furniture to the host of the "Green Wreath Inn," had been the cause of several ponderous blows dealt and received by Dumnoff, had produced the violent fall, upon a hard board floor, of a porter and two policemen and had ultimately brought the Count to prison for the night. Its value had become very great, for it had been paid for twice over, once by the man from whom it had been stolen, by the forfeiture of his caution money, and once by Fischelowitz in the sum of fifty marks lent to an adventurer; furthermore, the Count had solemnly pledged his word as a gentleman to pay for it a third time on the morrow, he having in his worldly possession the sum of one silver mark and two German pennies at the time of entering into the engagement. The actual sum of money paid and promised to be paid on the body of the now ruined Gigerl, now amounted, with interest, to more than four times its original value, thus constituting one of those interesting problems in real and comparative value so interesting to the ingenuous political economist, who believes that all value can be traced to supply and demand. Now, although the Gigerl was but a single doll, the supply of him, so to speak, had been surprisingly abundant, and the demand, if represented by the desire of any one person concerned to possess him, may be represented by the smallest of zeros. The consideration of so intricate a question belongs neither to the inventor of fiction nor to the historian of facts, and may therefore be abandoned to the political economist, who may, perhaps, be said to partake of the nature of both while possessing the virtues of neither.

The Count was in prison, therefore, on the eve of his return to splendour, and his companion in captivity was Dumnoff the mujik. They found themselves in a well-ventilated room, having high grated windows, through which the stars were visible, and dimly lighted by a small gas flame which burned in a lantern of white ground glass. The place was abundantly, if not luxuriously, furnished with flat wooden pallets, each having at the head a slanting piece of board supposed to do duty for a pillow. Outside the open door a policeman paced the broad passage, a man taken from the mounted detachment and whose scabbard and spurs clattered and jingled, hour after hour, as he walked. The sound produced something half rhythmical, like a broken tune in search of itself, and the change of sentinels made no perceptible difference in the regular nature of the unceasing noise.

Dumnoff, relieved of his handcuffs, stretched himself upon the pallet assigned to him, clasped his hands under the back of his head, and stared at the ceiling. The Count sat upon the edge of his board, crossing one knee over the other and looking at his nails, or trying to look at them in the insufficient light. In some distant part of the building a door was occasionally opened and shut, and the slight concussion sent long echoes down the stone passages. The Count sighed audibly.

"It is not so bad, after all," remarked Dumnoff. "I did not expect to end the evening so comfortably."

"It is bad enough," said the Count. He produced a crumpled piece of newspaper which contained a little tobacco, and rolled a cigarette thoughtfully. "It is bad enough," he repeated as he began to smoke.

"It would have been very easy to get away, if you had done like that brute of a Schmidt who ran away and left us."

"I do not think Schmidt is a brute," observed the other, blowing a huge ring of white smoke out into the dusk.

"I did not think so either. But I had arranged it all very well for you to get away—only you would not. You see, by an accident, the key was outside the door, so I kicked the people back and locked it. It would have taken a quarter of an hour for them to open it, and if you had only jumped—"

He turned his head, and glanced at the Count's spare, sinewy figure.

"You are light, too," he continued, "and you could not have hurt yourself. I cannot understand why you stayed."

"Dumnoff, my friend," said the Count, gravely, "we look at things in a different way. It is my duty to tell you that I think you behaved in the most honourable manner, under the circumstances, and I am deeply indebted to you for the gallant way in which you came back to stand by me, when you were yourself free. In a nobler warfare, such an action would have been rewarded with a cross of honour, as it truly deserved. It is true, as well, that you were not so intimately connected with the main question at stake, as I was, since it was I who was suspected of being in possession of unlawfully gotten goods. You were consequently, I think, at liberty to take your freedom if you could get it, without consulting your conscience further. Now my position was, and is, very different. I do not speak of any personal prejudice against the mere act of running away, considered as an immediate means of escape from disagreeable circumstances, with the hope of ultimate immunity from all unpleasant consequences. That is a matter of early education."

"I had very little early education," observed Dumnoff. "And none at all afterwards."

"My friend, it is not for you and me to enter into the history of our misfortunes. We have met in the vat of poverty to be seethed alike in the brew of unhappiness. We have sat at the same daily labour, we have shared often the same fare, but there is that in each of us which we can keep sacred from the contamination of confidence, and which will withstand even the thrusts of poverty. I mean our individual selves, the better part of us, the nobler element which has suffered, as distinguished from the grosser, which may yet enjoy. But I am wandering a little. I am afraid I sometimes do. I return to the point. For me to take advantage of your generous attempt to free me would have been to act as though I had a moral cause for flight. In other words, it would have been to acknowledge that I had committed some dishonourable action."

"It seems to me that to get away would have been the best way out of it. They would not have caught you if you had trusted to me, and if they did not catch you they could not prove anything against you."

"The suspicion would have remained, and the disgrace in my own eyes," answered the Count. "The question of physical fear is very different. I have been told that it depends upon the nerves and the action of the heart, and that courage is greatly increased by the presence of nourishment in the stomach. The same cannot be said of moral bravery, which proceeds more from the fear of seeming contemptible in our own eyes than from the wish to seem honourable in the estimation of others."

"I daresay," said Dumnoff, who was growing sleepy and who understood very little of his companion's homily.

"Precisely," replied the latter. "And yet even the question of physical courage is very complicated in the present case. It cannot be said, for instance, that you ran away from physical fear, after giving proof of such astonishing physical superiority. Your deeds this evening make the labours of Hercules dwindle to the proportions of mere mountebank's tricks."

"Was anybody badly injured?" asked Dumnoff, suddenly aroused by the pleasing recollections of the contest.

"I believe not seriously; I think I saw everybody whom you upset get on his feet sooner or later."

"Well," said Dumnoff with a sigh, "it cannot be helped. I did my best."

"I should think that you would be glad," suggested the Count. "You showed your prowess without any fatal result."

"Anything for a change in this dull life," grumbled the peasant with an air of dissatisfaction.

"With such a prospect of immediate change before me, I suppose I ought not to blame your longing for excitement. Nevertheless I consider it fortunate that nothing worse happened."

"You might take me with you to Russia," said Dumnoff, with a short laugh. "That would be an excitement, at least."

"After the way in which you have stood by me this evening, I will not refuse you anything. If you wish it, I will take you with me. I take it for granted that you are not prevented by any especial reason from entering our country."

"Not that I am aware of," laughed Dumnoff. "Do you know how I got to Germany? A gentleman from our part of the country brought me with him as coachman. One day the horses ran away in Baden-Baden, and he turned me out of the house."

"That was very inconsiderate of him," observed the Count.

"It is true that both the horses were killed," said Dumnoff, thoughtfully. "And the prince broke his arm, and the carriage was in good condition for firewood, and possibly I was a little gay—just a little—though I was so much upset by the accident that I could not remember exactly what happened before. Still—"

"Your conduct on that particular day seems to have left much to be desired," remarked the Count with some austerity.

"It has been my bad luck to be in a great many accidents," said the other. "But that one was remarkable. As far as I can recollect, we drove into the Grand Duke's four-in-hand on one side and drove out of it on the other. I never drove through a Grand Duke's equipage on any other occasion. It was lucky that his Serenity did not happen to be in it just at the time. There you have my history in a nutshell. As you say you will take me with you, I thought you ought to know."

"Certainly, certainly," answered the Count, vaguely. "I will take you with me—but not as coachman, I think, Dumnoff. We may find some more favourable sphere for your great physical strength."

"Anything you like. It is a good joke to dream of such a journey, is it not? Especially when one is locked up for the night in the police-station."

"It is certainly a relief to contemplate the prospect of such a change to-morrow," said the Count, his expression brightening in the gloom.

For a few moments there was silence between the two men. Dumnoff's small eyes fixed themselves on the shadowy outlines of his companion's face, as though trying to solve a problem far too complicated for his dull intellect.

"I wonder whether you are really mad," he said slowly, after a prolonged mental effort.

The Count started slightly and stared at the ex-coachman with a frightened look.

"Mad?" he repeated, nervously. "Who says I am mad? Why do you ask the question?"

"Most people say so," replied the other, evidently without any intention of giving pain. "Everybody who works with us thinks so."

"Everybody? Everybody? I think you are dreaming, Dumnoff. What do you mean?"

"I mean that they think so because you have those queer fits of believing yourself a rich count every week, from Tuesday night till Thursday morning. Schmidt was saying only yesterday to poor Vjera—"

"Vjera? Does she believe it too?" asked the Count in an unsteady voice, not heeding the rest of the speech.

"Of course," said Dumnoff, carelessly. "Schmidt was saying to me only yesterday that you were going to have a worse attack of it than usual because you were so silent."

"Vjera, too!" repeated the Count in a low voice. "And no one ever told me—" He passed his hand over his eyes.

"Tell me"—Dumnoff began in the tone of jocular familiarity which he considered confidential—"tell me—the whole thing is just a joke of yours to amuse us all, is it not? You do not really believe that you are a count, any more than I really believe that you are mad, you know. You do not act like a madman, except when you let the police catch you and lock you up for the night, instead of running away like a sensible man."

The Count's face grew bright again all at once. In the present state of his hopes no form of doubt seemed able to take a permanent hold of him.

"No, I am not mad," he said. "But on the other hand, Dumnoff, it is my conviction that you are exceedingly drunk. No other hypothesis can account for your very singular remarks about me."

"Oh, I am drunk, am I?" laughed the peasant. "It is very likely, and in that case I had better go to sleep. Good-night, and do not forget that you are to take me with you to Russia."

"I will not forget," said the Count.

Dumnoff stretched his heavy limbs on the wooden pallet, rolled his great head once or twice from side to side until his fur-like hair made something like a cushion and then, in the course of three minutes, fell fast asleep.

The Count sat upright in his place, drumming with his fingers upon one knee.

"It is a wonder that I am not mad," he said to himself. "But Vjera never thought it of me—and that fellow is evidently the worse for liquor."

CHAPTER VI

Johann Schmidt had not fled from the scene of action out of any consideration for his personal safety. He was, indeed, a braver man than Dumnoff, in proportion as he was more intelligent, and though of a very different temper, by no means averse to a fight if it came into his way. He had foreseen what was sure to happen, and had realised sooner than any one else that the only person who could set everything straight was Fischelowitz himself. So soon as he was clear of pursuit, therefore, he turned in the direction of the tobacconist's dwelling, walking as quickly as he could where there were many people and running at the top of his speed through such empty by-streets as lay in the direct line of his course. He rushed up the three flights of steps and rang sharply at the door.

Akulina's unmistakable step was heard in the passage a moment later. Schmidt would have preferred that Fischelowitz should have come himself, though he managed to live on very good terms with Akulina. Though far from tactful he guessed that in a matter concerning the Count, the tobacconist would prove more obliging than his wife.

"What is the matter?" inquired the mistress of the house, opening the door wide after she had recognised the Cossack in the feeble light of the staircase, by looking through the little hole in the panel.

"Good-evening, Frau Fischelowitz," said Schmidt, trying to appear as calm and collected as possible. "I would like to speak to your husband upon a little matter of business."

"He is not at home yet. I left him in the shop."

Almost before the words were out of her mouth, Schmidt had turned and was running down the stairs, two at a time. Akulina called him back.

"Wait a minute!" she cried, advancing to the hand-rail on the landing. "What in the world are you in such a hurry about?"

"Oh—nothing—nothing especial," answered the man, suddenly stopping and looking up.

Akulina set her fat hands on her hips and held her head a little on one side. She had plenty of curiosity in her composition.

"Well, I must say," she observed, "for a man who is not in a hurry about anything, you are uncommonly brisk with your feet. If it is only a matter of business, I daresay I will do as well as my husband."

"Oh, I daresay," admitted Schmidt, scratching his head. "But this is rather a personal matter of business, you see."

"And you mean that you want some money, I suppose," suggested Akulina, at a venture.

"No, no, not at all—no money at all. It is not a question of money." He hoped to satisfy her by a statement which was never without charm in her ears. But Akulina was not satisfied; on the contrary, she began to suspect that something serious might be the matter, for she could see Schmidt's face better now, as he looked up to her, facing the gaslight that burned above her own head. Having been violently angry not more than an hour or two earlier, her nerves were not altogether calmed, and the memory of the scene in the shop was still vividly present. There was no knowing what the Count might not have done, in retaliation for the verbal injuries she had heaped upon him, and her quick instinct connected Schmidt's unusually anxious appearance and evident haste to be off, with some new event in which the Count had played a part.

"Have you seen the Count?" she inquired, just as Schmidt was beginning to move again.

"Yes," answered the latter, trying to assume a doubtful tone of voice. "I believe—in fact, I did see him—for a moment—"

Akulina smiled to herself, proud of her own acuteness.

"I thought so," she said. "And he has made some trouble about that wretched doll—"

"How did you guess that?" asked Schmidt, turning and ascending a few steps. He was very much astonished.

"Oh, I know many things—many interesting things. And now you want to warn my husband of what the Count has done, do you not? It must be something serious, since you are in such a hurry. Come in, Herr Schmidt, and have a glass of tea. Fischelowitz will be at home in a few minutes, and you see I have guessed half your story, so you may as well tell me the other half and be done with it. It is of no use for you to go to the shop after him. He has shut up by this time, and you cannot tell which way he will come home, can you? Much better come in and have a glass of tea. The samovar is lighted and everything is ready, so that you need not stay long."

Schmidt lingered doubtfully a moment on the stairs. The closing hour was certainly past in early-closing Munich, and he might miss the tobacconist in the street. It seemed wiser to wait for him in his house, and so the Cossack reluctantly accepted the invitation, which, under ordinary circumstances, he would have regarded as a great honour. Akulina ushered him into the little sitting-room and prepared him a large glass of tea with a slice of lemon in it. She filled another for herself and sat down opposite to him at the table.

"The poor Count!" she exclaimed. "He is sure to get himself into trouble some day. I suppose people cannot help behaving oddly when they are mad, poor things. And the Count is certainly mad, Herr Schmidt."

"Quite mad, poor man. He has had one of his worst attacks to-day."

"Yes," assented the wily Akulina, "and if you could have seen him and heard him in the shop this evening—" She held up her hands and shook her head.

"What did he do and say?"

"Oh, such things, such things! Poor man, of course I am very sorry for him, and I am glad that my husband finds room to employ him, and keep him from starving. But really, this evening he quite made me lose my temper. I am afraid I was a little rough, considering that he is sensitive. But to hear the man talk about his money, and his titles, and his dignities, when he is only just able to keep body and soul together! It is enough to irritate the seven archangels, Herr Schmidt, indeed it is! And then at the same time there was that dreadful Gigerl, and my head was splitting—I am sure there will be a thunder-storm to-night—altogether, I could not bear it any longer, and I actually upset the Gigerl out of anger, and it rolled to the floor and was broken. Of course it is very foolish to lose one's temper in that way, but after all, I am only a weak woman, and I confess it was a relief to me when I saw the poor Count take the thing away. I hope I did not really hurt his feelings, for he is an excellent workman, in spite of his madness. What did he say, Herr Schmidt? I would so like to know how he took it. Of course he was very angry. Poor man, so mad, so completely mad on that one point!"

"To tell the truth," said Schmidt, who had listened attentively, "he did not like what you said to him at all."

"Well, really, was it my fault, Herr Schmidt? I am only a woman, and I suppose I may be excused if I lose my temper once in a year or so. It is very wearing on the nerves. Every Tuesday evening begins the same old song about the fortune and letters, and the journey to Russia. One gets very tired of it in the long-run. At first it used to amuse me."

"Do you think that Herr Fischelowitz can have gone anywhere else instead of coming home?" asked the Cossack, finishing the glass of tea, which he had swallowed burning hot out of sheer anxiety to get away.

"Oh no, indeed," cried Akulina in a tone of the most sincere conviction. "He always tells me where he is going. You have no idea what a good husband he is, and what a good man—though I daresay you know that after being with us so many years. Now, I am sure that if he had the least idea that anything had happened to the poor Count, he would run all the way home in order to hear it as soon as possible."

"No more tea, thank you, Frau Fischelowitz," said Schmidt, but she took his glass with a quiet smile and shredded a fresh piece of lemon into it and filled it up again, quite heedless of his protest. Schmidt resigned himself, and thanked her civilly.

"Of course," she said, presently, as she busied herself with the arrangements of the samovar, "of course it is nothing so very serious, is it? I daresay the Count has told you that he would not work any more for us, and you are anxious to arrange the matter? In that case, you need have no fear. I am always ready to forgive and forget, as they say, though I am only a weak woman."

"That is very kind of you," observed Schmidt, with a glitter in his eyes which Akulina did not observe.

"I guessed the truth, did I not?"

"Not exactly. The trouble is rather more serious than that. The fact is, as we were at supper, a man at another table saw the Gigerl in our hands and swore that it had been stolen from him some months ago."

"And what happened then?" asked Akulina with sudden interest.

"I suppose you may as well know," said Schmidt, regretfully. "There was a row, and the man made a great deal of trouble and at last the police were called in, and I came to get Herr Fischelowitz himself to come and prove that the Gigerl was his. You see why I am in such a hurry."

"Do you think they have arrested the Count?"

"I imagine that every one concerned would be taken to the police-station."

"And then?"

"And then, unless the affair is cleared up, they will be kept there all night."

"All night!" exclaimed Akulina, holding up her hands in real or affected horror. "Poor Count! He will be quite crazy, now, I fear—especially as this is Tuesday evening."

"But he must be got out at once!" cried Schmidt in a tone of decision. "Herr Fischelowitz will surely not allow—"

"No indeed! You have only to wait until he comes home, and then you can go together. Or better still, if he does not come back in a quarter of an hour, and if he has really shut up the shop as usual, you might look for him at the Café Luitpold, and if he is not there, it is just possible that he may have looked in at the Gärtner Platz Theatre, for which he often has free tickets, and if the performance is over—I fancy it is, by this time he may be in the Café Maximilian, or he may have gone to drink a glass of beer in the Platzl, for he often goes there, and—well, if you do not find him in any of those places—"

"But, good Heavens, Frau Fischelowitz, you said you were quite sure he was coming home at once! Now I have lost all this time!"

Schmidt had risen quickly to his feet, in considerable anxiety and haste. Akulina smiled good-humouredly.

"You see," she said, "it is just possible that to-night, as he was a little annoyed with me for being sharp with the Count, he may have gone somewhere without telling me. But I really could not foresee it, because he is such a very good—"

"I know," interrupted the Cossack. "If I miss him, you will tell him, will you not? Thank you, and good-night, Frau Fischelowitz, I cannot afford to wait a moment longer."

So saying Johann Schmidt made for the door and got out of the house this time without any attempt on the part of his amiable hostess to detain him further. She had indeed omitted to tell him that her last speech was not merely founded on a supposition, since Fischelowitz had really been very much annoyed and had declared that he would not come home but would spend the evening with a friend of his who lived in the direction of Schwabing, one of the suburbs of Munich farthest removed from the places in which she advised Schmidt to make search.

The stout housewife disliked and even detested the Count for many reasons all good in her own eyes, among which the chief one was that she did dislike him. She felt for him one of those strong and invincible antipathies which trivial and cunning natures often feel for very honourable and simple ones. To the latter the Count belonged, and Akulina was a fine specimen of the former. If the Count had been literally starving and clothed in rags, he would have been incapable of a mean thought or of a dishonest action. Whatever his origin had been, he had that, at least, of a nobility undeniable in itself. That his character was simple in reality, may as yet seem less evident. He was regarded as mad, as has been seen, but his madness was methodical and did not overstep certain very narrow bounds. Beyond those limits within which others, at least, did not consider him responsible, his chief idea seemed to be to gain his living quietly, owing no man anything, nor refusing anything to any man who asked it. This last characteristic, more than any other, seemed to prove the possibility of his having been brought up in wealth and with the free use of money, for his generosity was not that of the vulgar spendthrift who throws away his possessions upon himself quite as freely as upon his companions. He earned enough money at his work to live decently well, at least, and he spent but the smallest sum upon his own wants. Nevertheless he never had anything to spare for his own comfort, for he was as ready to give a beggar in the street the piece of silver which represented a good part of the value of his day's work as most rich people are to part with a penny. He never inquired the reason for the request of help, but to all who asked of him he gave what he had, gravely, without question, as a matter of course. If Dumnoff's pockets were empty and his throat dry, he went to the Count and got what he wanted. Dumnoff might be brutal, rude, coarse; it made no difference. The Count did not care to know where the money went nor when it would be returned, if ever. If Schmidt's wife—for he had a wife—was ill, the Count lent all he had, if the children's shoes were worn out, he lent again, and when Schmidt, who was himself extremely conscientious in his odd way, brought the money back, the Count generally gave it to the first poor person whom he met. Akulina supposed that this habit belonged to his madness. Others, who understood him better, counted it to him for righteousness, and even Dumnoff, the rough peasant, showed at times a friendly interest in him, which is not usually felt by the unpunctual borrower towards the uncomplaining lender.

But Akulina could understand none of these things. She belongs by nature to the class of people whose first impulse on all occasions is to say: "Money is money." There can be no mutual attraction of intellectual sympathy between these, and those other persons who despise money in their hearts, and would rather not touch it with their hands. It has been seen also that the events connected with the Gigerl's first appearance in the shop had been of a nature to irritate Akulina still more. The dislike nourished in her stout bosom through long months and years now approached the completion of its development, and manifested itself as a form of active hatred. Akulina was delighted to learn that there was a prospect of the Count's spending the night in the police-station and she determined that Johann Schmidt should not find her husband before the next day, and that when the partner of her bliss returned—presumably pacified by the soothing converse of his friend—she would not disturb his peace of mind by any reference to the Count's adventures. It was therefore with small prospect of success that the Cossack began his search for Fischelowitz.

Only a man who has sought anxiously for another, all through the late evening, in a great city, knows how hopeless the attempt seems after the first hour. The rapid motion through many dusky streets, the looking in, from time to time, upon some merry company assembled in a warm room under a brilliant light, the anxious search among the guests for the familiar figure, the disappointment, as each fancied resemblance shows, on near approach, a face unknown to the searcher, the hurried exit and the quick passage through the dark night air to the next halting-place—all these impressions, following hurriedly upon each other, confuse the mind and at last discourage hope.

Schmidt did not realise how late it was, when, abandoning his search for his employer, he turned towards the police-station in the hope of still rendering some assistance to his friend. He could not gain admittance to the presence of the officer in charge, however, and was obliged to content himself with the assurance that the Count had been treated "with consideration," as the phrase was, and that there would be plenty of time for talking in the morning. The policemen in the guard-room were sleepy and not disposed to enter into conversation. Schmidt turned his steps in the direction of the tobacconist's house for the second time, in sheer despair. But he found the street door shut and the whole house was dark. Nevertheless, he pulled the little handle upon which, by the aid of a flickering match, he discovered a figure of three, corresponding to the floor occupied by Fischelowitz. Again and again he tugged vigorously at the brass knob until he could hear the bell tinkling far above. No other sound followed, however, in the silence of the night, though he strained his ears for the faintest echo of a distant footfall and the slightest noise indicating that a window or a door was about to be opened. He wondered whether Fischelowitz had come home. If he had, Akulina had surely told him the story of the evening, and he would have been heard of at the police-station, for it was incredible that he should let the night pass without making an effort to liberate the Count. Therefore the tobacconist had in all probability not yet returned. The night was fairly warm, and the Cossack sat down upon a doorstep, lighted a cigarette and waited. In spite of long years spent in the midst of German civilisation, it was still as natural to him to sit down in the open air at night and to watch the stars, as though he had never changed his own name for the plain German appellation of Johann Schmidt, nor laid aside the fur cap and the sheepskin coat of his tribe for the shabby jacket and the rusty black hat of higher social development.

There was no truth in Akulina's statement that a thunder-storm was approaching. The stars shone clear and bright, high above the narrow street, and the solitary man looked up at them, and remembered other days and a freer life and a broader horizon; days when he had been younger than he was now, a life full of a healthier labour, a horizon boundless as that of the little street was limited. He thought, as he often thought when alone in the night, of his long journeys on horseback, driving great flocks of bleating sheep over endless steppes and wolds and expanses of pasture and meadow; he remembered the reddening of the sheep's woolly coats in the evening sun, the quick change from gold to grey as the sun went down, the slow transition from twilight to night, the uncertain gait of his weary beast as the darkness closed in, the soft sound of the sheep huddling together, the bark of his dog, the sudden, leaping light of the camp-fire on the distant rising ground, the voices of greeting, the bubbling of the soup kettle, the grateful rest, the song of the wandering Tchumák—the pedlar and roving newsman of the Don. He remembered on holidays the wild racing and chasing and the sports in the saddle, the picking up of the tiny ten-kopek bit from the earth at a full gallop, the startling game in which a row of fearless Cossack girls join hands together, daring the best rider to break their rank with his plunging horse if he can, the mad laughter of the maidens, the snorting and rearing of the animal as he checks himself before the human wall that will not part to make way for him. All these things he recalled, the change of the seasons, the iron winter, the scorching summer, the glory of autumn and the freshness of spring. Born to such a liberty, he had fallen into the captivity of a common life; bred in the desert, he knew that his declining years would be spent in the eternal cutting of tobacco in the close air of a back shop; trained to the saddle, he spent his days seated motionless upon a wooden chair. The contrast was bitter enough, between the life he was meant to lead by nature, and the life he was made to lead by circumstances. And all this was the result in the first instant of a girl's caprice, of her fancy for another man, so little different from himself that a Western woman could hardly have told the two apart. For this, he had left the steppe, had wandered westward to the Dnieper and southward to Odessa, northward again to Kiew, to Moscow, to Nizni-Novgorod, back again to Poland, to Krakau, to Prague, to Munich at last. Who could remember his wanderings, or trace the route of his endless journeyings? Not he himself, surely, any more than he could explain the gradual steps by which he had been transformed from a Don Cossack to a German tobacco-cutter in a cigarette manufactory.

But his past life at least furnished him with memories, varied, changing, full of light and life and colour, wherewith to while away an hour's watching in the night. Still he sat upon his doorstep, watching star after star as it slowly culminated over the narrow street and set, for him, behind the nearest house-top. He might have sat there till morning had he not been at last aware that some one was walking upon the opposite pavement.

His quick ear caught the soft fall of an almost noiseless footstep and he could distinguish a shadow a little darker than the surrounding shade, moving quickly along the wall. He rose to his feet and crossed the street, not believing, indeed, that the newcomer could be the man he wanted, but anxious to be fully satisfied that he was not mistaken. He found himself face to face with a young girl, who stopped at the street door of the tobacconist's house, just as he reached it. Her head was muffled in something dark and he could not distinguish her features. She started on seeing him, hesitated and then laid her hand upon the same knob which Schmidt had pulled so often in vain.

"It is of no use to ring," he said, quietly. "I have given it up."

"Herr Schmidt!" exclaimed the girl in evident delight. It was Vjera.

"Yes—but, in Heaven's name, Vjera, what are you doing here at this hour of the night? You ought to be at home and asleep."

"Oh, you have not heard the dreadful news," cried poor Vjera in accents of distress. "Oh, if we cannot get in here, come with me, for the love of Heaven, and help me to get him out of that horrible place—oh, if you only knew what has happened!"

"I know all about it, Vjera," answered the Cossack. "That is the reason why I am here. I was with them when it happened and I ran off to get Fischelowitz. As ill luck would have it, he was out."

In a few words Schmidt explained the whole affair and told of his own efforts. Vjera was breathless with excitement and anxiety.

"What is to be done? Dear Herr Schmidt! What is to be done?" She wrung her hands together and fixed her tearful eyes on his.

"I am afraid that there is nothing to be done until morning—"

"But there must be something, there shall be something done! They will drive him mad in that dreadful place—he is so proud and so sensitive—you do not know—the mere idea of being in prison—"

"It is not so bad as that," answered Schmidt, trying to reassure her. "They assured me that he was treated with every consideration, you know. Of course that means that he was not locked up like a common prisoner."

"Do you think so?" Vjera's tone expressed no conviction in the matter.

"Certainly. And it shows that he is not really suspected of anything serious—only, because Fischelowitz could not be found—"

"But he is there—there in his house, asleep!" cried Vjera. "And we can wake him up—of course we can. He cannot be sleeping so soundly as not to hear if we ring hard. At least his wife will hear and look out of the window."

"I am afraid not. I have tried it."

But Vjera would not be discouraged and laid hold of the bell-handle again, pulling it out as far as it would come and letting it fly back again with a snap. The same results followed as when Schmidt had made the same attempt. There was a distant tinkling followed by total silence. Vjera repeated the operation.

"You cannot do more than I have done," said her companion, leaning his back against the door and watching her movements.

"I ought to do more."

"Why, Vjera?"

"Because he is more to me than to you or to any of the rest," she answered in a low voice.

"Do you mean to say that you love the Count?" inquired Schmidt, surprised beyond measure by the girl's words and rendered thereby even more tactless than usual.

But Vjera said nothing, having been already led into saying more than she had wished to say. She pulled the bell again.

"I had never thought of that," remarked the Cossack in a musing tone. "But he is mad, Vjera, the poor Count is mad. It is a pity that you should love a madman—"

"O, don't, Herr Schmidt—please don't!" cried Vjera, imploring him to be silent as much with her eyes as with her voice.

"No, but really," continued the other, as though talking to himself, "there are things that go beyond all imagination in this world. Now, who would ever have thought of such a thing?"

This time Vjera did not make any answer, nor repeat her request. But as she tugged with all her might at the brass handle, the Cossack heard a quick sob, and then another.

"Poor Vjera!" he exclaimed kindly, and laying his hand on her shoulder. "Poor child! I am very sorry for you, poor Vjera—I would do anything to help you, indeed I would—if I only knew what it should be."

"Then help me to wake up Fischelowitz," answered the girl in a shaken voice. "I am sure he is at home at this time—"

"I have done all I can. If he will not wake, he will not. Or if he is awake he will not put his head out of the window, which is much the same thing so far as we are concerned. By the bye, Vjera, you have not told me how you came to hear of the row. It is queer that you should have heard of it—"

"Herr Homolka—you know, my landlord—had seen the Count go by with the Gigerl and the policemen. He asked some one in the crowd and learned the story. But it was late when he came home, and he told us—I was sitting up sewing with his wife—and then I ran here. But do please help me—we can do something, I am sure."

"I do not see what, short of climbing up the flat walls of the house. But I am not a lizard, you know."

"We might call. Perhaps they would hear our voices if we called together," suggested Vjera, drawing back into the middle of the street and looking up at the closed windows of the third story.

"Herr Fischelowitz!" she cried, in a shrill, weak tone that seemed to find no echo in the still air.

"Herr Fischelowitz, Fischelowitz, Fischelowitz!" bawled the Cossack, taking up the idea and putting it into very effective execution. His brazen voice, harsh and high, almost made the windows rattle.

"Somebody will hear that," he observed and cleared his throat for another effort.

A number of persons heard it, and at the first repetition of the yell, two or three windows were angrily opened. A head in a white nightcap looked out from the first story.

"What do you want at this hour of the night?" asked the owner of the nightcap, already in a rage.

"I want Herr Fischelowitz, who lives in this house," answered the Cossack, firmly.

"Do you live here? Are you shut out?"

"No—we only want—"

"Then go to the devil!" roared the infuriated German, shutting his window again with a vicious slam. A grunt of satisfaction from other directions was followed by the shutting of other windows, and presently all was silent again.

"I am afraid they sleep at the back of the house," said Vjera, growing despondent at last.

"I am afraid so, too," answered Johann Schmidt, proudly conscious that the noise he had made would have disturbed the slumbers of the Seven Sleepers of Ephesus.

CHAPTER VII

"You had better let me take you home," said Schmidt, kindly, after the total failure of the last effort.

Vjera seemed to be stupefied by the sense of disappointment. She went back to the door of the tobacconist's house and put out her hand as though to ring the bell again then, realising how useless the attempt would be, she let her arms fall by her sides and leaned against the door-post, her muffled head bent forward and her whole attitude expressing her despair.

"Come, come, Vjera," said the Cossack in an encouraging tone, "it is not so bad after all. By this time the Count is fast asleep and is dreaming of his fortune, you know, so that it would be a cruelty to wake him up. In the morning we will all go with Fischelowitz and have him let out, and he will be none the worse."

"I am afraid he will be—very much the worse," said Vjera. "It is Wednesday to-morrow, and if he wakes up there—oh, I do not dare think of it. It will make him quite, quite mad. Can we do nothing more? Nothing?"

"I think we have done our best to wake up this quarter of the town, and yet Fischelowitz is still asleep. No one else can be of any use to us—therefore—" he stopped, for his conclusion seemed self-evident.

"I suppose so," said Vjera, regretfully. "Let us go, then."

She turned and with her noiseless step began to walk slowly away, Schmidt keeping close by her side. For some minutes neither spoke. The streets were deserted, dry and still.

"Do you think there is any truth at the bottom of the Count's story?" asked the Cossack at last.

"I do not know," Vjera answered, shaking her head. "I do not know what to think," she continued after a little pause. "He tells us all the same thing, he speaks of his letters, but he never shows them to anyone. I am afraid—" she sighed and stopped speaking.

"I will tell you this much," said her companion. "That man is honest to the backbone, honest as the good daylight on the hills, where there are no houses to darken it and make shadows."

"He is an angel of goodness and kindness," said Vjera softly.

"I know he is. Is he not always helping others when he is starving himself? Now what I say is this. No man who is as good and as honest as he is, can have become so mad about a mere piece of fancy—about an invented lie, to be plain. What there is in his story I do not know, but I am sure that there was truth in it once. It may have been a long time ago, but there was a time once, when he had some reason to expect the money and the titles he talks of every Tuesday evening."

"Do you really think that?" asked Vjera, eagerly. Her own understanding had never gone so far in its deduction.

"I am sure of it. I know nothing about mad people, but I am sure that no honest man ever invented a story out of nothing and then became crazy because it did not turn out true."

"But you, who have travelled so much, Herr Schmidt, have you ever heard the name before—have you ever heard of such a family?"

"I have a bad memory for names, but I believe I have. I cannot be sure. It makes no difference. It is a good Russian name, in any case, and a gentleman's name, I should think. Of course I only mean that I—that you should not think that because I—in fact," blundered out the good man, "you must not suppose that you will be a real countess, you know."

"I?" exclaimed Vjera, with a nervous, hysterical laugh, which the Cossack supposed to be genuine.

"That is all I wanted to say," he continued in a tone of relief, as though he felt that he had done his duty in warning the poor girl of a possible disappointment. "It may be true—of course, and I am sure that it once was, or something like it, but I do not believe he has any chance of getting his own after so long."

"I cannot think of it—in either way. If it is all an old forgotten tale which he believes in still-why then, he is mad. Is it not dreadful to see? So quiet and sensible all the week, and then, on Tuesday night, his farewell speech to us all—every Tuesday—and his disappointment the next day, and then a new week begun without any recollection of it all! It is breaking my heart, Herr Schmidt!"

"Indeed, poor Vjera, you look as though it were."

"And yet, and yet—I do not know. I think that if it were one day to turn out true—then my heart would be quite broken, for he would go away, and I should never see him again."

Accustomed as she was to daily association with the man who was walking by her side, knowing his good heart and feeling his sympathy, it is small wonder that the lonely girl should have felt impelled to unburden her soul of some of its bitterness. If her life had gone on as usual, undisturbed by anything from without, the confessions which now fell from her lips so easily would never have found words. But she had been unsettled by what had happened in the early evening, and unstrung by her great anxiety for the Count's safety. Her own words sounded in her ear before she knew that she was going to speak them.

"I am sure that something dreadful is going to happen," she continued after a moment's pause. "He will go mad in that horrible prison, raving mad, so that they will have to—to hold him—" she sobbed and then recovered herself by an effort. "Or else—he will fall ill and die, after it—" Here she broke down completely and stopping in the middle of the street began crying bitterly, clutching at Schmidt's arm as though to keep from falling.

"I should not wonder," he said, but she fortunately did not catch the words.

He was very sorry for the poor girl, and felt inclined to take her in his arms and carry her to her home, for he saw that she was weak and exhausted as well as overcome by her anxiety. Before resorting to such a measure, however, he thought it best to try to encourage her to walk on.

"Nothing that one expects, ever happens," he said confidently, and passing his arm through hers, as though to lead her away. "Come, you will be at home presently and then you will go to bed and in the morning, before you are at the shop, everything will have been set right, and I daresay the Count will be there before you, and looking as well as ever."

"How can you say that, when you know that he never comes on Wednesdays!" exclaimed Vjera through her tears. "I am sure something dreadful will happen to him. No, not that way—not that way!"

Schmidt was trying to guide her round a sharp corner, but she resisted him.

"But that is the way home," protested the Cossack.

"I know, but I cannot go home, until I have seen where he is. I must go—you must not prevent me!"

"To the police-station?" inquired Schmidt in considerable astonishment. "They will not let us go in, you know. You cannot possibly see him. What good can it do you to go and look at the place?"

"You do not understand, Herr Schmidt! You are good and kind, but you do not understand me. Pray, pray come with me, or let me go alone. I will go alone, if you do not want to come. I am not at all afraid—but I must go."

"Well, child," answered Schmidt, good-humouredly. "I will go with you, since you are so determined."

"Is this the way? Are you not misleading me? Oh, I am sure I shall never see him again—quick, let us walk quickly, Herr Schmidt! Only think what he may be suffering at this very moment!"

"I am sure he is asleep, my dear child. And when we are outside of the police-station we cannot know what is going on inside, whether our friend is asleep or awake, and it can do no good whatever to go. But since you really wish it so much, we are going there as fast as we can, and I promise to take you by the shortest way."

Her step grew more firm as they went on and he felt that there was more life in the hand that rested on his arm. The prospect of seeing the walls of the place in which the Count was unwillingly spending the night gave Vjera fresh strength and courage. The way was long, as distances are reckoned in Munich, and more than ten minutes elapsed before they reached the building. A sentry was pacing the pavement under the glare of the gaslight, his shadow lengthening, shortening, disappearing and lengthening again on the stone-way as he walked slowly up and down. Vjera and her companion stopped on the other side of the street. The sentinel paid no attention to them.

"You are quite sure it is there?" asked the girl, under her breath. Schmidt nodded instead of answering.

"Then I will pray that all may be well this night," she said.

She dropped the Cossack's arm and slipped away from him; then pausing at a little distance, in the deep shadow of an archway opposite the station, she knelt down upon the pavement, and taking some small object, which was indistinguishable in the darkness, from the bosom of her frock she clasped her hands together and looked upwards through the gloom at the black walls of the great building. The Cossack looked at her in a sort of half-stupid, half-awed surprise, scarcely understanding what she was doing at first, and feeling his heart singularly touched when he realised that she was praying out here in the street, kneeling on the common pavement of the city, as though upon the marble floor of a church, and actually saying prayers—he could hear low sounds of earnest tone escaping from her lips—prayers for the man she loved, because he was shut up for the night in the police-station like an ordinary disturber of the peace. He was touched, for the action, in its simplicity of faith, set in vibration the chords of a nature accustomed originally to simple things, simple hopes, simple beliefs. Instinctively, as he watched her, Johann Schmidt raised his hat from his round head for a moment, and if he had possessed any nearer acquaintance with praying in general or with any prayer in particular it is almost certain that his lips would have moved. As it was, he felt sorry for Vjera, he hoped that the Count would be none the worse for his adventure, and he took off his hat. Let it be counted to him for righteousness.

As for poor Vjera herself, she was so much in earnest that she altogether forgot where she was. For love, it has been found, is a great suggester of prayer, if not of meditation, and when the beloved one is in danger a little faith seems magnified to such dimensions as would certainly accept unhesitatingly a whole mountain of dogmas. Vjera's ideas were indeed confused, and she would have found it hard to define the result which she so confidently expected. But if that result were to be in any proportion to her earnestness of purpose and sincerity of heart, it could not take a less imposing shape than a direct intervention of Providence, at the very least; and as the poor Polish girl rose from her knees she would hardly have been surprised to see the green-coated sentinel thrust aside by legions of angelic beings, hastening to restore to her the only treasure her humble life knew of, or dreamed of, or cared for.

But as the visions which her prayers had called before her faded away into the night, she saw again the dingy walls of the hated building, the gilt spike on the helmet of the policeman and the shining blade that caught the light as he moved on his beat. For one moment Vjera stood quite still. Then with a passionate gesture she stretched out both arms before her, as though to draw out to herself, by sheer strength of longing, the man whose life she felt to be her own—and at last, wearied and exhausted, but no longer despairing altogether, she covered her face with her hands and repeated again and again the two words which made up the burden of her supplication.

"Save him, save him, save him!" she whispered to herself.

When she looked up, at last, Schmidt was by her side. There was something oddly respectful in his attitude and manner as he stood there awaiting her pleasure, ready to be guided by her whithersoever she pleased. It seemed to him that on this evening he had begun to see Vjera in a new light, and that she was by no means the poor, insignificant little shell-maker he had always supposed her to be. It seemed to him that she was transformed into a woman, and into a woman of strong affections and brave heart. And yet he knew every outline of her plain face, and had known every change of her expression for years, since she had first come to the shop, a mere girl not yet thirteen years of age. Nor had it been from lack of observation that he had misunderstood her, for like most men born and bred in the wilderness, he watched faces and tried to read them. The change had taken place in Vjera herself and it must be due, he thought, to her love for the poor madman. He smiled to himself in the dark, scarcely understanding why. It was strange to him perhaps that madness on the one side should bring into life such a world of love on the other.

Vjera turned towards him and once more laid her hand upon his arm.

"Thank you," she said. "I could not have slept if I had not come here first, and it was very good of you. I will go home, but do not come with me—you must be tired."

"I am never tired," he answered, and they began to walk away in the direction whence they had come.

For a long time neither spoke. At last Schmidt broke the silence.

"Vjera," he said, "I have been thinking about it all and I do not understand it. What kind of love is it that makes you act as you do?"

Vjera stood still, for they were close to her door, and there was a street lamp at hand so that she could see his face. She saw that he asked the question earnestly.

"It is something that I cannot explain—it is something holy," she answered.

Perhaps the forlorn little shell-maker had found the definition of true love.

She let herself in with her key and Schmidt once more found himself alone in the street. If he had followed his natural instinct he would have loitered about in one of the public squares until morning, making up for the loss of his night's rest by sleeping in the daytime. But he had taken upon himself the responsibilities of marriage as they are regarded west of the Dnieper, and his union had been blessed by the subsequent appearance of a number of olive-branches. It was therefore necessary that he should sleep at night in order to work by day, and he reluctantly turned his footsteps towards home. As he walked, he thought of all that had happened since five o'clock in the afternoon, and of all that he had learned in the course of the night. Vjera's story interested him and touched him, and her acts seemed to remind him of something which he nevertheless could not quite remember. Far down in his toughened nature the strings of a forgotten poetry vibrated softly as though they would make music if they dared. Far back in the chain of memories, the memory once best loved was almost awake once more, the link of once clasped hands was almost alive again, the tender pressure of fingers now perhaps long dead was again almost a reality able to thrill body and soul. And with all that, and with the certainty that those things were gone for ever, arose the great longing for one more breath of liberty, for one more ride over the boundless steppe, for one more draught of the sour kvass, of the camp brew of rye and malt.

The longing for such things, for one thing almost unattainable, is in man and beast at certain times. In the distant northern plains, a hundred miles from the sea, in the midst of the Laplander's village, a young reindeer raises his broad muzzle to the north wind, and stares at the limitless distance while a man may count a hundred. He grows restless from that moment, but he is yet alone. The next day, a dozen of the herd look up, from the cropping of the moss, snuffing the breeze. Then the Laps nod to one another, and the camp grows daily more unquiet. At times, the whole herd of young deer stand at gaze, as it were, breathing hard through wide nostrils, then jostling each other and stamping the soft ground. They grow unruly and it is hard to harness them in the light sledge. As the days pass, the Laps watch them more and more closely, well knowing what will happen sooner or later. And then at last, in the northern twilight, the great herd begins to move. The impulse is simultaneous, irresistible, their heads are all turned in one direction. They move slowly at first, biting still, here and there, at the bunches of rich moss. Presently the slow step becomes a trot, they crowd closely together while the Laps hasten to gather up their last unpacked possessions, their cooking utensils and their wooden gods. The great herd break together from a trot to a gallop, from a gallop to a break-neck race, the distant thunder of their united tread reaches the camp during a few minutes, and they are gone to drink of the polar sea. The Laps follow after them, dragging painfully their laden sledges in the broad track left by the thousands of galloping beasts—a day's journey, and they are yet far from the sea, and the trail is yet broad. On the second day it grows narrower, and there are stains of blood to be seen; far on the distant plain before them their sharp eyes distinguish in the direct line a dark, motionless object, another and then another. The race has grown more desperate and more wild as the stampede neared the sea. The weaker reindeer have been thrown down, and trampled to death by their stronger fellows. A thousand sharp hoofs have crushed and cut through hide and flesh and bone. Ever swifter and more terrible in their motion, the ruthless herd has raced onward, careless of the slain, careless of food, careless of any drink but the sharp salt water ahead of them. And when at last the Laplanders reach the shore their deer are once more quietly grazing, once more tame and docile, once more ready to drag the sledge whithersoever they are guided. Once in his life the reindeer must taste of the sea in one long, satisfying draught, and if he is hindered he perishes. Neither man nor beast dare stand between him and the ocean in the hundred miles of his arrow-like path.

Something of this longing came upon the Cossack, as he suddenly remembered the sour taste of the kvass, to the recollection of which he had been somehow led by a train of thought which had begun with Vjera's love for the Count, to end abruptly in a camp kettle. For the heart of man is much the same everywhere, and there is nothing to show that the step from the sublime to the ridiculous is any longer in the Don country than in any other part of the world. But between poor Johann Schmidt and his draught of kvass there lay obstacles not encountered by the reindeer in his race for the Arctic Ocean. There was the wife, and there were the children, and there was the vast distance, so vast that it might have discouraged even the fleet-footed scourer of the northern snows. Johann Schmidt might long for his kvass, and draw in his thin, wan lips at the thought of the taste of it, and bend his black brows and close his sharp eyes as in a dream—it was all of no use, there was no change in store for him. He had cast his lot in the land of beer and sausages, and he must work out his salvation and the support of his family without a ladleful of the old familiar brew to satisfy his unreasonable caprices.

So, last of all those concerned in the events of the evening, Johann Schmidt went home to bed and to rest. That power, at least, had remained with him. Whenever he lay down he could close his eyes and be asleep, and forget the troubles and the mean trifles of his thorny existence. In this respect he had the advantage of the others.

Vjera lay down, indeed, but the attempt to sleep seemed more painful than the accepted reality of waking. The night was the most terrible in her remembrance, filled as it was with anxiety for the fate of the man she so dearly loved. To her still childlike inexperience of the world, the circumstances seemed as full of fear and danger as though the poor Count had been put upon his trial for a murder or a robbery on an enormous scale, instead of being merely detained because he could not give a satisfactory account of a puppet which had been found in his possession. In the poor girl's imagination arose visions of judges, awful personages in funereal robes and huge Hack caps, with cruel lips and hard, steely eyes, sitting in solemn state in a gloomy hall and dispensing death, disgrace, or long terms of prison, at the very least, to all comers. For her, the police-station was a dungeon, and she fancied the Count chained to a dank and slimy wall in a painful position, chilled to the marrow by the touch of the dripping stone, his teeth chattering, his face distorted with suffering. Of course he was in a solitary cell, behind a heavy door, braced with clamps and bolts and locks and studded with great dark iron nails. Without, the grim policemen were doubtless pacing up and down with drawn swords, listening with a murderous delight to the groans of their victim as he writhed in his chains. In the eyes of the poor and the young, the law is a very terrible thing, taking no account of persons, and very little of the relative magnitude of men's misdeeds. The province of justice, as Vjera conceived it, was to crush in its iron claws all who had the misfortune to come within its reach. Vjera had never heard of Judge Jeffreys nor of the Bloody Assizes, but the methods of procedure adopted by that eminent destroyer of his kind would have seemed mild and humane compared with what she supposed that all men, innocent or guilty, had to expect after they had once fallen into the hands of the policeman. She was not a German girl, taught in the common school to understand something of the methods by which society governs itself. Her early childhood had been spent in a Polish village, far within the Russian frontier, and though the law in Russian Poland is not exactly the irresponsible and blood-thirsty monster depicted by young gentlemen and old maids who traverse the country in search of horrors, yet it must be admitted by the least prejudiced that it sometimes moves in a mysterious way, calculated to rouse some apprehension in the minds of those who are governed by it. And Vjera had brought with her her childish impressions, and applied them in the present case as descriptive of the Munich police-station. The whole subject was to her so full of horror that she had not dared to ask Schmidt for the details of the Count's situation. To her, a revolutionary caught in the act of undermining the Tsar's bedroom, could not be in a worse case. She would not have believed Schmidt, had he told her that the Count was sitting in an attitude of calm thought upon the edge of a broad wooden bench, his hands quite free from chains and gyves, and occupied in rolling cigarettes at regular intervals of half an hour—and this, in a clean and well-ventilated room, lighted by a ground glass lantern. She would have supposed that Schmidt was inventing a description of such comfort and comparative luxury in order to calm her fears, and she would have been ten times more afraid than before.

It is small wonder that she could not sleep. The Count's arrest alone would have sufficed to keep her in an agony of wakefulness, and there were other matters, besides that, which tormented the poor girl's brain. She had been long accustomed to his singular madness and to hearing from him the assurance of his returning to wealth. At first, with perfect simplicity, she had believed every word of the story he told with such evident certainty of its truth, and she had reproached her older companions, as far as she dared, for their incredulity. But at last she had herself been convinced of his madness as through the weeks, and months, and years, the state of expectation returned on Tuesday evenings, to be followed by the disappointments of Wednesday and by the oblivion which ensued on Thursday morning. Vjera, like the rest, had come to regard the regularly recurring delusion as being wholly groundless, and not to be taken into account, except inasmuch as it deprived them of the Count's company on Wednesdays, for on that day he stayed at home, in his garret room, waiting for the high personages who were to restore to him his wealth. Sometimes, indeed, when he chanced to be very sure that they would not come for him until evening, he would stroll through the town for an hour, looking into the shop windows and making up his mind what he should buy; and sometimes, on such occasions, he would visit the scene of his late labours, as he called the tobacconist's shop on that day of the week, and would exchange a few friendly words with his former companions. On Thursday morning he invariably returned to his place without remark and resumed his work, not seeming to understand any observations made about his absence or strange conduct on the previous day.

So far the story he had told Vjera had always been the same. Now, however, he had introduced a new incident in the tale, which filled poor Vjera with dismay. He had never before spoken of his father and brother, except as the causes of his disasters, explaining that the powerful influence of his own friends, aided by the machinery of justice, had at last obliged them to concede him a proportional part of the fortune. Fischelowitz was accustomed to laugh at this statement, saying that if the Count were only a younger son, the law would do nothing for him and that he must continue to earn his livelihood as he could. In the course of a long time Vjera had come to the conclusion, by comparing this remark with the Count's statement when in his abnormal condition, that he was indeed the son of a great noble who had turned him out of doors for some fancied misdeed, and from whom he had in reality nothing to expect. Such was the girl's present belief.

Now, however, he had suddenly declared that his father and his brother were dead. With a woman's keenness she took alarm at this new development. She really loved the poor man with all her heart. If this new addition to his story were a mere invention, it was a sign that his madness was growing upon him, and she had heard her companions discuss their comrade often enough to know that, in their opinion, if he began to grow worse, he would very soon be in the madhouse. It was bad enough to go through what she suffered so often, to see the inward struggle expressed on his face, whenever he chanced to be alone with her on a Tuesday afternoon, to hear from his lips the same assurance of love, the same offer of marriage, and to know that all would be forgotten and that his manner to her would change again, by Thursday, to that of a uniform, considerate kindness. It was bad enough, for the girl loved him and was sensitive. But it would be worse—how much worse, she dared not think—to see him go mad before her very eyes, to see him taken away at last from the midst of them all to the huge brick house in the outskirts of the city beyond the Isar.

One more hypothesis remained. This time the story might turn out true. She believed in his birth and in his misfortunes, and in the existence of his father and his brother. They might indeed be dead, as he had told her, and he would then, perhaps, be sole master in their stead—she did not know how that would be, in Russia. But then, if it were all true, he must go away—and her life would be over, with its loving hope and its hopeless love.

It is small wonder that Vjera did not sleep that night.

CHAPTER VIII

Once or twice in the course of the night, the Count changed his position, got up, stretched himself and paced the length of the room. Dumnoff lay like a log upon his pallet, his head thrown back, his mouth open, snoring with the strong bass vibration of a thirty-two-foot organ pipe. The Count looked at him occasionally, but did not envy him his power of sleep. His own reflections were in a measure more agreeable than any dream could have been, certainly more so in his judgment than the visions of unlimited cabbage soup, vodka, and fighting which were doubtless delighting Dumnoff's slumbering soul.

As the church clocks struck one hour after another, his spirits rose. He had, indeed, never had the least apprehension concerning his own liberty, since he knew himself to be perfectly innocent. He only desired to be released as soon as possible in order to repair the damage done to his coat and collar before the earliest hour at which the messengers of good news could be expected at his house. Meanwhile he cared little whether he spent the night on a bench in the police-station, or on one of the rickety wooden chairs which afforded the only sitting accommodation in his own room. He could not sleep in either case, for his brain was too wide awake with the anticipations of the morrow, and with the endless plans for future happiness which suggested themselves.

At last he was aware that the nature of the light in the room was changing and that the white ground glass of the lantern was illuminated otherwise than by the little flame within. The high window, as he looked up, was like a grey figure cut out of dark paper, and the dawn was stealing in at last.

"Wednesday at last!" he exclaimed softly to himself. "Wednesday at last!" A gentle smile spread over his tired face, and made it seem less haggard and drawn than it really was.

The day broke, and somewhere not far from the window, the birds all began to sing at once, filling the room with a continuous strain of sound, loud, clear and jubilant. The soft spring air seemed to awake, as though it had itself been sleeping through the still night and must busy itself now in sending the sweet breezes upon their errands to the flowers.

"I always thought it would come in spring," thought the Count, as he listened to the pleasant sounds, and then held one of his yellow hands up to the window to feel the freshness that was without.

He wondered how long it would be before Fischelowitz would come and tell the truth of the Gigerl's story. By his knowledge of the time of daybreak, he guessed that it was not yet much past four o'clock, and he doubted whether Fischelowitz would come before eight. The tobacconist was a kind man, but a comfortable one, loving his rest and his breakfast and his ease at all times. Moreover, as the Count knew better than any one else, Akulina would be rejoiced to hear of the misadventure which had befallen her enemy and would in no way hurry her husband upon his mission of justice. She would doubtless consume an unusual amount of time in the preparation of his coffee, she would presumably tell him that the milkman had not appeared punctually, and would probably assert that there were as yet no rolls to be had. The immediate consequence of these spiteful fictions would be that Fischelowitz would dress himself very leisurely, swallowing the smoke of several cigarettes in the meanwhile, and that he would hardly be clothed, fed and out of the house before eight in the morning, instead of being on the way to the shop at seven as was his usual practice.

But the Count was not at all disturbed by this. The persons whose coming he expected were not of the class who pay visits at eight o'clock. It was as pleasant to sit still and think of the glorious things in the future, as to do anything else, until the great moment came. Here, at least, he was undisturbed by the voices of men, unless Dumnoff's portentous snore could be called a voice, and to this his ear had grown accustomed.

He sat down again, therefore, in his old position, crossed one knee over the other and again produced the piece of crumpled newspaper which held his tobacco. The supply was low, but he consoled himself with the belief that Dumnoff probably had some about him, and rolled what remained of his own for immediate consumption.

He was quite right in his surmises concerning his late employer and the latter's wife. Akulina had in the first place let her husband sleep as long as he pleased, and had allowed a considerable time to elapse before informing him of the events of the previous evening. As was to be expected, the good man stated his intention of immediately procuring the Count's liberation, and was only prevailed upon with difficulty to taste his breakfast. One taste, however, convinced him of the necessity of consuming all that was set before him, and while he was thus actively employed Akulina entered into the consideration of the theft, recalling all the details she could remember about the intimacy supposed to exist between the Count and the swindler in coloured glasses, and conscientiously showing the matter in all its aspects.

"One fact remains," she said, in conclusion, "he promised you upon his honour last night that he would pay you the fifty marks to-day, and, in my opinion, since he has been the means of your losing the Gigerl after all, he ought to be made to pay the money."

"And where can he get fifty marks to pay me?" inquired Fischelowitz with careless good-humour.

"Where he got the doll, I suppose," said Akulina, triumphantly completing the vicious circle in which she caused her logic to move.

Fischelowitz smiled as he pushed away his cup, rose and lighted a fresh cigarette.

"You are a very good housekeeper, Akulina, my love," he observed. "You always know how the money goes."

"That is more than can be said for some people," laughed Akulina. "But never mind, Christian Gregorovitch, your wife is only a weak woman, but she can take care for two, never fear!"

Fischelowitz was of the same opinion as he, at last, took his hat and left the house. To him, the whole affair had a pleasant savour of humour about it, and he was by no means so much disturbed as Johann Schmidt or Vjera. He had lived in Munich many years and understood very well the way in which things are managed in the good-natured Bavarian capital. A night in the police-station in the month of May seemed by no means such a terrible affair, certainly not a matter involving any great suffering to any one concerned. Moreover it could not be helped, a consideration which, when available, was a great favourite with the rotund tobacconist. Whatever the Count had done on the previous night, he said to himself, was done past undoing; and though, if he had found Akulina awake when he returned from spending the evening with his friend, and if she had then told him what had happened, he would certainly have made haste to get the Count released—yet, since Akulina had been sound asleep, he had necessarily gone to bed in ignorance of the story, to the temporary inconvenience of the arrested pair.

He was not long in procuring an order for the Count's release, but Dumnoff's case seemed to be considered as by far the graver of the two, since he had actually been guilty of grasping the sacred, green legs of two policemen, at the time in the execution of their duty, and of violently turning the aforesaid policemen upside down in the public room of an eating-house. It was, indeed, reckoned as favourable to him that he had returned and submitted to being handcuffed without offering further resistance, but it might have gone hard with him if Fischelowitz had not procured the co-operation of a Munich householder and taxpayer to bail him out until the inquiry should be made. It would have been a serious matter for Fischelowitz to lose the work of Dumnoff in his "celebrated manufactory" for any length of time together, since it was all he could do to meet the increasing demands for his wares with his present staff of workers.

"And how did you spend the night, Count?" he inquired as they walked quickly down the street together. Dumnoff had made off in the opposite direction, in search of breakfast, after which he intended to go directly to the shop, as though nothing had happened.

"I spent it very pleasantly, thank you," answered the Count. "The fact is that, with such an interesting day before me, I should not have slept if I had been at home. I have so much to think of, as you may imagine, and so many preparations to make, that the time cannot seem long with me."

"I am glad of that," said Fischelowitz, serenely. "I suppose we shall not see you to-day?"

"Hardly—hardly," replied the Count, as though considering whether his engagements would allow him to look in at the shop. "You will certainly see me this evening, at the latest," he added, as if he had suddenly recollected something. "I have not forgotten that I am to hand you fifty marks—I only regret that you should have lost the Gigerl, which, I think I have heard you say, afforded you some amusement. However, the money shall be in your hands without delay, or with as little delay as possible. My friends will in all probability arrive by the mid-day train and will, of course, come to me at once. An hour or so to talk over our affairs, and I shall then have leisure to come to you for a few moments and to settle that unfortunate affair. Not indeed, my dear Herr Fischelowitz, that I have ever held myself responsible for the dishonest young man who wore green spectacles. I was, indeed, a loser by him myself, in an insignificant sum, and as he turned out to be such an indifferent character, I do not mind acknowledging the fact. I do not think it can harm him, if I do. No. I was not responsible for him to you, but since your excellent wife, Frau Fischelowitz, labours under the impression that I was, I am quite willing to accept the responsibility, and shall therefore discharge the debt before night, as a matter of honour."

"It is very kind of you," remarked the tobacconist, smiling at the impressive manner in which the promise was made. "But of course, Count, if anything should prevent the arrival of your friends, you will not consider this to be an engagement."

"Nothing will prevent the coming of those I expect, nor, if anything could, would such an accident prevent my fulfilling an engagement which, since your excellent wife's remarks last night, I do consider binding upon my honour. And now, Herr Fischelowitz, with my best thanks for your intervention this morning, I will leave you. After the vicissitudes to which I have been exposed during the last twelve hours, my appearance is not what I could wish it to be. I have the pleasure to wish you a very good morning."

Shaking his companion heartily by the hand, the Count bowed civilly and turned into an unfrequented street. Fischelowitz looked after him a few seconds, as though expecting that he would turn back and say something more, and then walked briskly in the direction of his shop.

He found Akulina standing at the door which led into the workroom, in such a position as to be able to serve a customer should any chance to enter, and yet so placed as to see the greater part of her audience. For she was holding forth volubly in her thick, strong voice, giving her very decided opinion about the events of the previous evening, the Count, considered in the first place as a specimen of the human race, and secondly, as in relation to his acts. Her hearers were poor Vjera, her insignificant companion and the Cossack who listened, so to say, without enthusiasm, unless the occasional foolish giggle of the younger girl was to be taken for the expression of applause.

"I am thoroughly sick of his crazy ways," she was saying, "and if he were not really such a good workman we should have turned him out long ago. But he really does make cigarettes very well, and with the new shop about to be opened, and the demand there is already, it is all we can do to keep people satisfied. Not but what my husband has been talking lately of getting a new workman from Vilna, and if he turns out to be all that we expect, why the Count may go about his business and we shall be left in peace at last. Indeed it is high time. My poor nerves will not stand many more such scenes as last night, and as for my poor husband, I believe he has lost as much money through the Count and his friends as he has paid to him for work, and if you turn that into figures it makes the cigarettes he rolls worth six marks a thousand instead of three, which is more than any pocket can stand, while there are children to be fed at home. And if you have anything to say to that, little husband, why just say it!"

Fischelowitz had entered the shop and the last words were addressed to him.

"Oh, nothing, nothing," he answered, beginning to bustle cheerily about the place, setting a box straight here, removing an empty one there, opening the till and counting the small change, and, generally, doing all those things which he was accustomed to do when he appeared in the morning.

Poor Vjera looked paler and more waxen than ever in her life before, so pale indeed was she that the total absence of colour lent a sort of refinement to her plain features, not often found even in really beautiful faces. She had suffered intensely and was suffering still. From the first words that Akulina had spoken she had understood that the Count had been in the station-house all night, and she found herself reviewing all the hideous visions of his cruel treatment which she had conjured up since the previous evening. Akulina of course hastened to say that Fischelowitz had lost no time in having the poor man set at liberty, and this at least was a relief to Vjera's great anxiety. But she wanted to hear far more than Akulina could or would tell, she longed to know whether he had really suffered as she fancied he had, and how he looked after spending in a prison the night that had seemed so long to her. She would have given anything to overwhelm the tobacconist with questions, to ask for a minute description of the Count's appearance, to express her past terrors to some one and to have some one tell her that they had been groundless.

But she dared not open her lips to speak of the matters which filled her thoughts. She was so wretchedly nervous that she felt as though the tears would break out at the sound of her own voice, and at the same time she was disturbed by the consciousness that Johann Schmidt's eyes watched her closely from the corner in which he was steadily wielding his swivel knife. It had been almost natural to tell him of her love in the darkness of the streets, in the mad anxiety for the loved one's safety, in the weariness and the hopelessness of the night hours. But now, sitting at her little table, at her daily work, with all the trivial objects that belonged to it recalling her to the reality of things, she realised that her day-dreams were no longer her secret, and she was ashamed that any one should guess the current of her thoughts. It was hard for her to understand how she could have thus taken the Cossack into her confidence, and she would have made almost any sacrifice to take back the confession. Good he was, and honest, and kind-hearted, but she was ashamed of what she had done. It seemed to her that, besides giving up to another the knowledge of her heart, she had also done something against the dignity of him she loved. She herself felt no superiority over Johann Schmidt; they were equals in every way. But she did feel, and strongly, that the Cossack was not the equal of the Count, and she reproached herself with having made a confidant of one beneath her idol in station and refinement. This feeling sprang from such a multiplicity of sources, as almost to defy explanation. There was, at the bottom of it, the strange, unreasoning notion of the superiority of one class over another by right of blood, from which no race seems to be wholly exempt, and which has produced such surprising results in the world. Poor Vjera had been brought up in one of those countries where that tradition is still strongest. The mere sound of the word "Count" evoked a body of impressions so firmly rooted, so deeply ingrained, as necessarily to influence her judgment. The outward manner of the man did the rest, his dignity under all circumstances, his uncomplaining patience, his unquestioning generosity, his quiet courtesy to every one. There was something in every word he spoke, in his every action, which distinguished him from his companions. They themselves felt it. He was sometimes ridiculous, poor man, and they laughed together over his carefully chosen language, over the grand sweep of his bow and his punctilious attention to the smallest promise or shadow of a promise. These things amused them, but at the same time they felt that he could never be what they were, and that those manners and speeches of his, which, if they had imitated them, would have seemed in themselves so many forms of vulgarity, were somehow not vulgar in him. Vjera, as she loved him, felt all this far more keenly than the others. And besides, to add to her embarrassment at present, there was the girl's maidenly shyness and timidity. Since she had told Johann Schmidt her secret, she felt as though all eyes were upon her, and as though every one were about to turn upon her with those jesting questions which coarse natures regard as expressions of sympathy where love is concerned. And yet no one spoke to her, nor disturbed her. There was only the disquieting consciousness of the Cossack's curious scrutiny to remind her that all things were not as they had been yesterday.

The hours of the morning seemed endless. On all other days, Vjera was accustomed to see the Count's quiet face opposite to her, and when she was most weary of her monotonous toil, a glance at him gave her fresh courage, and turned the currents of her thoughts into a channel not always smooth indeed, but long familiar and never wearisome to follow. The stream emptied, it is true, into the dead sea of doubt, and each time, as she ended the journey of her fancy, she felt the cruel chill of the conclusion, as though she had in reality fallen into a deep, dark water; but she was always able to renew the voyage, to return to the fountain-head of love, enjoying at least the pleasant, smooth reaches of the river, that lay between the racing rapids and the tumbling falls.

But to-day there was no one at the little table opposite, and Vjera's reflections would not be guided in their familiar course. Her heart yearned for the lonely man who, on that day, sat in the solitude of his poor chamber confidently expecting the messengers of good tidings who never came. She wondered what expression was on his face, as he watched the door and listened for the fall of feet upon the stairs. She knew, for she knew his nature, that he had carefully dressed himself in what he had that was best, in order to receive decently the long-expected visit; she fancied that he would move thoughtfully about the narrow room, trying to give it a feebly festive look in accordance with his own inward happiness. He would forget to eat, as he sat there, hearing the hours chime one after another, seeing the sun rise higher and higher until noon and watching the lengthening shadows of the chimneys on the roofs as day declined. More than all, she wondered what that dreadful moment could be like when, each week, he gave up hope at last, and saw that it had all been a dream. She had seen him more than once, towards the evening of the regularly recurring day, still confidently expecting the coming of his friends, explaining that they must come by the last train, and hastening away in order to be ready to receive them. Somewhere between the Wednesday evening and the Thursday morning there must be an hour, of which she hardly dared to think, in which all was made clear to him, or in which a veil descended over all, shutting out in merciful obscurity the brilliant vision and the bitter disappointment. If she could only be with him at that moment, she thought, she might comfort him, she might make his sufferings more easy to bear, and at the idea the tears that were so near rose nearer still to the flowing, kept back only by shame of being seen.

It was a terrible day, and everything jarred upon the poor girl's nature, from Akulina's thick, strong voice, continually discussing the question of marks and pennies, with occasional allusions to late events, to the disagreeable, scratching, paring sound of the Cossack's heavy knife as it cut its way through the great packages of leaves. The mid-day hour afforded no relief, for the pressure of work was great and each of the workers had brought a little food to be eaten in haste and almost without a change of position. For the work was paid for in proportion to its quantity, and the poor people were glad enough when there was so much to do, since there was then just so much more to be earned. There were times when the demand was slack and when Fischelowitz would not keep his people at their tables for more than two or three hours in a day. They might occupy the rest of their time as they could, and earn something in other ways, if they were able. When those hard times came poor Vjera picked up a little sewing, paid for at starvation rates, Johann Schmidt turned his hand to the repairing of furs, in which he had some skill, and which is an art in itself, and Dumnoff varied his existence by exercising great economy in the matter of food without making a similar reduction in the allowance of his drink. Under ordinary circumstances Vjera would have rejoiced at the quantity of work to be done, and as it was, her mental suffering did not make her fingers awkward or less nervously eager in the perpetual rolling of the little pieces of paper round the glass tube. Even acute physical pain is often powerless to affect the mechanical skill of a hand trained for many years to repeat the same little operation thousands of times in a day with unvarying perfection. Vjera worked as well and as quickly as ever, though the hours seemed so endlessly long as to make her wonder why she did not turn out more work than usual. From time to time the two men exchanged more or less personal observations after their manner.

"It seems to me that you work better than usual," remarked the Cossack, looking at Dumnoff.

"I feel better," laughed the latter. "I feel as though I had been having a holiday and a country dance."

"For the sake of your health, you ought to have a little excitement now and then," continued Schmidt. "It is hard for a man of your constitution to be shut up day after day as you are here. A little bear-fight now and then would do you almost as much good as an extra bottle of brandy, besides being cheaper."

"Yes." Dumnoff yawned, displaying all his ferocious white teeth to the assembled company. "That is true—and then, those green cloth policemen look so funny when one upsets them. I wish I had a few here."

"You have not heard the last of your merry-making yet," said Fischelowitz, who was standing in the doorway. "If I had not got you out this morning you would still be in the police-station."

"There is something in that," observed Schmidt. "If he were not out, he would still be in."

"Well, if I were, I should still be asleep," said Dumnoff. "That would not be so bad, after all."

"You may be there again before long," suggested Fischelowitz. "You know there is to be an inquiry. I only hope you will do plenty of work before they lock you up for a fortnight."

"I suppose they will let me work in prison," answered Dumnoff, indifferently. "They do in some places."

Vjera, whose ideas of prisons have been already explained at length, was so much surprised that she at last opened her lips.

"Have you ever been in prison?" she asked in a wondering tone.

"Several times," replied the other, without looking up. "But always," he added, as though suddenly anxious for his reputation, "always for that sort of thing—for upsetting somebody who did not want to be upset. It is a curious thing—I always do it in the same way, and they always tumble down. One would think people would learn—" he paused as though considering a profound problem.

"Perhaps they are not always the same people," remarked the Cossack.

"That is true. That may have something to do with it." The ex-coachman relapsed into silence.

"But, is it not very dreadful—in prison?" asked Vjera rather timidly after a short pause.

"No—if one can sleep well, the time passes very pleasantly. Of course, one is not always as comfortable as we were last night. That is not to be expected."

"Comfortable!" exclaimed the girl in surprise.

"Well—we had a nice room with a good light, and there happened to be nobody else in for the night. It was dry and clean and well furnished—rather hard beds, I believe, though I scarcely noticed them. We smoked and talked some time and then I went to sleep. Oh, yes—I passed a very pleasant evening, and a comfortable night."

"But I thought—" Vjera hesitated, as though fearing that she was going to say something foolish. "I thought that prisoners always had chains," she said, at last.

Everybody laughed loudly at this remark and the poor girl felt very much ashamed of herself, though the question had seemed so natural and had been in her mind a long time. It was an immense relief, however, to know that things had not been so bad as she had imagined, and Dumnoff's description of the place of his confinement was certainly reassuring.

As the endless day wore on, she began to glance anxiously towards the door, straining her ears for a familiar footstep in the outer shop. As has been said, the Count sometimes looked in on Wednesdays, when his calculations had convinced him that his friends, not having arrived by one train, could not be expected for several hours. But to-day he did not come, to-day when Vjera would have given heaven and earth for a sight of him. Never, in her short life, had she realised how slowly the hours could limp along from sunrise to noon, from noon to sunset, never had the little spot of sunlight which appeared in the back-shop on fine afternoons taken so long to crawl its diagonal course from the left front-leg of Dumnoff's table, where it made its appearance, to the right-hand corner of her own, at which point it suddenly went out and was seen no more, being probably intercepted by some fixed object outside.

Time is the measure of most unhapppiness, for it is in sorrow and anxiety that we are most keenly conscious of it, and are oppressed by its leaden weight. When we are absorbed in work, in study, in the production of anything upon which all our faculties are concentrated, we say that the time passes quickly. When we are happy we know nothing of time nor of its movement, only, long afterwards, we look back, and we say, "How short the hours seemed then!"

Vjera toiled on and on, watching the creeping sunshine on the floor, glancing at the ever-increasing heap of cut leaves that fell from the Cossack's cutting-block, noting the slow rise in the pile of paper shells before her and comparing it with that produced by the girl at her elbow, longing for the moment when she would see the freshly-made cigarettes just below the inner edge of Dumnoff's basket, taking account of every little thing by which to persuade herself that the day was declining and the evening at hand.

Her life was sad and monotonous enough at the best of times. It seemed as though the accidents of the night had made it by contrast ten times more sad and monotonous and hopeless than before.

CHAPTER IX

The Count, as Vjera supposed, had dressed himself with even greater care than usual in anticipation of the official visit, and while she was working through the never-ending hours of her weary day, he was calmly seated upon a chair by the open window in his little room, one leg crossed over the other, one hand thrust into the bosom of his coat and the other extended idly upon the table by his side. His features expressed the perfect calm and satisfaction of a man who knows that something very pleasant is about to happen, who has prepared himself for it, and who sits in the midst of his swept and garnished dwelling in an attitude of pleased expectancy.

The Count's face was tired, indeed, and there were dark circles under his sunken grey eyes, brought there by loss of sleep as much as by an habitual facility for forgetting to eat and drink. But in the eyes themselves there was a bright, unusual light, as though some brilliant spectacle were reflected in them out of the immediate future. There was colour, too, in his lean cheeks, a slight flush like that which comes into certain dark faces with the anticipation of any keen pleasure. As he sat in his chair, he looked constantly at the door of the room, as though expecting it to open at any moment. From time to time, voices and footsteps were heard on the stairs, far below. When any of these sounds reached him, the Count rose gravely from his seat, and stood in the middle of the room, slowly rubbing his hands together, listening again, moving a step to the one side or the other and back again, in the mechanical manner of a person to whom a visitor has been announced and who expects to see him appear almost immediately. But the footsteps echoed and died away and the voices were still again. The Count stood still a few moments when this happened, satisfying himself that he had been mistaken, and then, shaking his head and once more passing his hands round each other, he resumed his seat and his former attitude. He listened also for the chiming of the hours, and when he was sure that an hour had passed since the arrival of his imaginary express train, he rose again, looked out of the window, watched the wheeling of the house swallows, and assumed an air of momentary indifference. The next ringing of the clock bells revived the illusion. Another train was doubtless just running in to the station, and in a quarter of an hour his friends might be with him. There was no time to be lost. The flush returned to his cheeks as he hastily combed his smooth hair for the twentieth time, examining his appearance minutely in the dingy, spotted mirror, brushing his clothes—far too well brushed these many years—and lastly making sure that there was no weak point in the adjustment of his false collar. He made another turn of inspection round his little room, feeling sure that there was just time to see that all was right and in order, but already beginning to listen for a noise of approaching people on the stairs. Once more he straightened and arranged the patched coverlet of Turkey red cotton upon the bed, so that it should hide the pillows and the sheets; once more he adjusted the clean towel neatly upon the wooden peg over the washing-stand, discreetly concealing the one he had used in the drawer of the table; for the last time he made sure that the chair which had the broken leg was in such close and perfect contact with the wall as to make it safely serviceable if not rashly removed into a wider sphere of action. Then, as he passed the chest of drawers, he gave a final touch to the half-dozen ragged-edged books which composed his library—three volumes of Puschkin, of three different editions, Ivan Kryloff's *Poems and Fables*, Gogol's *Terrible Revenge*, Tolstoi's *How People Live*, and two or three more, including Koltsoff, the shepherd poet, and an ancient guide to the city of Kiew—as heterogeneous a collection of works as could be imagined, yet all notable in their way, except, indeed, the guide-book, for beauty, power, or touching truth.

And when he had touched and straightened everything in the room, he returned to his seat, calmly expectant as ever, to wait for the footsteps on the stairs, to rise and rub his hands, if the sound reached him, to shake his head gravely if he were again disappointed, in short to go through the same little round of performance as before until some chiming clock suggested to his imagination that the train had come and brought no one, and that he might enjoy an interval of distraction in looking out of the window until the next one arrived. The Count must have had a very exaggerated idea of the facility of communication between Munich and Russia, for he assuredly stood waiting for his friends, combed, brushed, and altogether at his best, more than twenty times between the morning and the evening. As the day declined, indeed, his imaginary railway station must have presented a scene of dangerous confusion, for his international express trains seemed to come in quicker and quicker succession, until he barely had time to look out of the window before it became necessary to comb his hair again in order to be ready for the next possible arrival. At last he walked perpetually on a monotonous beat from the window to the mirror, from the mirror to the door, and from the door to the mirror again.

Suddenly he stopped and tapped his forehead with his hand. The sun was setting and the last of his level rays shot over the sea of roofs and the forest of chimneys and entered the little room in a broad red stream, illuminating the lean, nervous figure as it stood still in the ruddy light.

"Good Heavens!" exclaimed the Count, in a tone of great anxiety, "I have forgotten Fischelowitz and his money."

There was a considerable break in the continuity of the imaginary time-table, for he stood still a long time, in deep thought. He was arguing the case in his mind. What he had promised was, to consider the fifty marks as a debt of honour. Now a debt of honour must be paid within twenty-four hours. No doubt, thought the Count, it would not be altogether impossible to consider the twenty-four hours as extending from midnight to midnight. The Russians have an expression which means a day and a night together—they call that space of time the sutki, and it is a more or less elastic term, as we say "from day to day," "from one evening to another." Rooms in Russian hotels are let by the sutki, railway tickets are valid for one or more sutki, and the Count might have chosen to consider that his sutki extended from the time when he had spoken to Fischelowitz until twelve o'clock on the following night. But he had no means of knowing exactly what the time had been when he had been in the shop, and his punctilious ideas of honour drove him to under-estimate the number of hours still at his disposal. Moreover, and this last consideration determined his action, if he brought the money too late it was to be feared that Fischelowitz would have shut up the shop, after which there would be no certainty of finding him. The Count wished to make the restitution of the money in Akulina's presence, but he was also determined to give the fifty marks directly to the tobacconist.

He saw that the sun was going down, and that there was no time to be lost. It occurred to him at the same instant that if he was to pay the debt at all, he must find money for that purpose, and although, in his own belief, he was to be master of a large fortune in the course of the evening, no scheme for raising so considerable a sum as fifty marks presented itself to his imagination. Poor as he was, he was far more used to lending than to borrowing, and more accustomed to giving than to either. He regretted, now, that he had bound himself to pay the debt to-day. It would have been so easy to name the next day but one. But who could have foreseen that his friends would miss that particular train and only arrive late in the evening?

He paced his room in growing anxiety, his trouble increasing in exact proportion with the decrease of the daylight.

"Fifty marks!" he exclaimed, in dismay, as he realised more completely the dilemma in which he was placed. "Fifty marks! It is an enormous sum to find at a moment's notice. If they had only telegraphed me a credit at once, I could have got it from a bank—a bank—yes—but they do not know me. That is it. They do not know me. And then, it is late."

The drops of perspiration stood on his pale forehead as he began to walk again. He glanced at his possessions and turned from the contemplation of them in renewed despair. Many a time, before, he had sought among his very few belongings for some object upon which a pawnbroker might advance five marks, and he had sought in vain. The furniture of the room was not his, and beyond the furniture the room contained little enough. He had parted long ago with an old silver watch, of which the chain had even sooner found its way to the lender's. A long-cherished ring had disappeared last winter, by an odd coincidence, at the very time when Johann Schmidt's oldest child was lying ill with diphtheria. As for clothing, he had nothing to offer. The secrets of his outward appearance were known to him alone, but they were of a nature to discourage the hope of raising money on coat or trousers. A few well-thumbed volumes of Russian authors could not be expected to find a brilliant sale in Munich at a moment's notice. He looked about, and he saw that there was nothing, and he turned very pale.

"And yet, before midnight, it must be paid," he said. Then his face brightened again. "Before midnight—but they will be here before then, of course. Perhaps I may borrow the money for a few hours."

But in order to do this, or to attempt it, he must go out. What if his friends arrived at the moment when he was out of the house?

"No," he said, consulting his imaginary time-table, "there is no train now, for a couple of hours, at least."

He took up his hat and turned to go. It struck him, however, that to provide against all possible accidents it would be as well to leave some written word upon his table, and he took up a sheet of writing paper and a pen. It was remarkable that there was a good supply of the former on the table, and that the inkstand contained ink in a fluid state, as though the Count were in the habit of using it daily. He wrote rapidly, in Russian.

"This line is to inform you that Count Skariatine is momentarily absent from his lodging on a matter of urgent importance, connected with a personal engagement. He will return as soon as possible and requests that you will have the goodness to wait, if you should happen to arrive while he is out."

He set the piece of notepaper upright, in a prominent position upon the table, and exactly opposite to the door. He did not indeed recollect that in the course of half an hour the room would be quite dark, and he was quite satisfied that he had taken every reasonable precaution against missing his visitors altogether. Once more he seized his hat, and a moment later he was descending the long flights of stairs towards the street. As he went, the magnitude of the sum of money he needed appalled him, and by the time he stepped out upon the pavement into the fresh evening air, he was in a state of excitement and anxiety which bordered on distraction. His brain refused to act any longer, and he was utterly incapable of thinking consecutively of anything, still less of solving a problem so apparently incapable of solution as was involved in the question of finding fifty marks at an hour's notice. It was practically of little use to repeat the words "Fifty marks" incessantly and in an audible voice, to the great surprise of the few pedestrians he met. It was far from likely that any of them would consider themselves called upon to stop in their walk and to produce two large gold pieces and a small one, for the benefit of an odd-looking stranger. And yet, as he hurried along the street, the poor Count had not the least idea where he was going, and if he should chance to reach any definite destination in his erratic course he would certainly be much puzzled to decide what he was to do upon his arrival. The one thing which remained clearly defined in his shaken intelligence was that he must pay to Fischelowitz the money promised within the limit of time agreed upon, or be disgraced for ever in his own eyes, as well as in the estimation of the world at large. The latter catastrophe would be bad enough, but nothing short of self-destruction could follow upon his condemnation of himself.

A special Providence is said to watch over the movements of madmen, sleep-walkers and drunkards. Those who find difficulty in believing in the direct intervention of Heaven in very trivial matters of everyday life, are satisfied to put a construction of less tremendous import upon the facts in cases concerning the preservation of their irresponsible brethren. A great deal may be accounted for by considering what are the instincts of the body when momentarily liberated from the directing guidance of the mind. It has been already noticed in the course of this story that, when the Count did not know where he was going, he was generally making the best of his way to the establishment in which so much of his time was passed. This is exactly what took place on the present occasion. Conscious only of his debt, and not knowing where to find money with which to pay it, he was unwittingly hurrying towards the very place in which the payment was to be made, and, within a quarter of an hour of his leaving his lodging, he found himself standing on the pavement, over against the tobacconist's shop, stupidly gazing at the glass door, the well-known sign and the familiar, dilapidated chalet of cigarettes which held a prominent place in the show window. No longer ago than yesterday afternoon the little Swiss cottage had been flanked by the Wiener Gigerl, whose smart red coat and insolent face had been the cause of so much disaster and anxiety during the past twenty-four hours. The very fact that the doll was no longer there, in its accustomed place, served to remind the Count of his rash promise to pay the money and dangerously increased the excitement which already possessed him. He wiped the cold drops from his brow and leaned for a moment against the brick wall behind him. He was dizzy, confused and tired.

The tormenting thought that was driving him recalled his failing consciousness of outer things. He straightened himself again and made a step forward, as though he would cross the street, but paused again before his foot had left the pavement. Then he asked of his senses how he had got to the place where he stood. He did not remember traversing the familiar highways and byways by which he was accustomed daily to make his way from his lodging to the shop. Every object on the way had long been so well known to him as to cause a permanent impression in his brain, which was distinctly visible to him whenever he thought of the walk in any way, whether he had just been over the ground or not. He could not now account to himself for his being so near Fischelowitz's shop, and he found it impossible to decide whether he had come thither by his usual route or not. It was still harder to explain the reason for his coming, since the fifty marks were no nearer to his hand than before, and without them it was useless to think of entering. As he stood there, hesitating and trying to grasp the situation more clearly, it grew, on the contrary, more and more confused. At the same time the bells of a neighbouring church struck the hour, and the clanging tone revived in his mind the other impression, which had possessed it all day, the impression that his friends were at that moment arriving at the railway station. The confusion in his thoughts became intolerable, and he covered his eyes with one hand, steadying himself by pressing the other against the wall.

He did not know how long he had stood thus, when an anxious voice recalled him to outer things—a voice in which love, sympathy, tenderness and anxiety for him had taken possession of the weak tones and lent them a passing thrill of touching music.

"In Heaven's name—what is it? Speak to me—I am Vjera—here, beside you."

He looked up suddenly, and seemed to recover his self-possession.

"You came just in time, Vjera—God bless you. I—" he hesitated. "I think—I must have been a little dizzy with the heat. It is a warm evening—a very warm evening."

He pressed an old silk pocket-handkerchief to his moist brow, the pocket-handkerchief which he always had about him, freshly ironed and smoothly folded, on the day when he expected his friends. Vjera, her face pale with distress, passed her arm through his and made as though she would walk with him down the gentle slope of the street, which leads in the direction of the older city. He suffered himself to be led a few steps in silence.

"Where are you going, Vjera?" he asked, stopping again and looking into her face.

"Wherever you like," she said, trying to speak cheerfully. She saw that something terrible was happening, and it was only by a desperate effort that she controlled the violent hysterical emotion that rose like a great lump in her throat.

"Ah, that is it, Vjera," he answered. "That is it. Where shall I go, child?" Then he laughed nervously. "The fact is," he continued, "that I am in a very absurd position. I do not at all know what to do."

Perhaps he had tried to give himself courage by the attempt to laugh, but, in that case, he had failed for the present. In spite of his words his despair was evident. His usually erect carriage was gone. His head sank wearily forward, his shoulders rounded themselves as though under a burden, his feet dragged a little as he tried to walk on again, and he leaned heavily on the young girl's arm.

"What is it?" she asked. "Tell me—perhaps I can help you—I mean—I beg your pardon," she added, humbly, "perhaps it would help you to speak of it. That sometimes makes things seem clearer just when they have been most confused."

"Perhaps so, Vjera, perhaps so. You are a very good girl, and you came just in time. I love you, Vjera—do not forget that I love you." His voice was by turns sharp and suddenly low and monotonous, like that of a man talking in sleep. Altogether his manner was so strange that poor Vjera feared the very worst. The extremity of her anxiety kept her from losing her self-possession. For the first time in her life she felt that she was the stronger of the two, and that if he was to be saved it must be by her efforts rather than by anything he was now able to do for himself. She loved him, mad or sane, with an admiration and a devotion which took no account of his intellectual state except to grieve over it for his own sake. The belief that in this crisis she might be of use to him, strongly conquered the rising hysterical passion, and drove the tears so far from her eyes that she wondered vaguely why she had been so near to shedding them a few moments sooner. She pressed his arm with her hand.

"And I, too, I love you, with all my heart and soul," she said. "And if you will tell me what has happened, I will do what I can—if it were my life that were needed. I know I can help you, for God will help me."

He raised his head a little and again stood still, gazing into her eyes with an odd sort of childish wonder.

"What makes you so strong, Vjera? You used to be a weak little thing."

"Love," she answered.

It was strange to see such a man, outwardly lean, tough-looking, well put together and active, though not, indeed, powerful, looking at the poor white-faced girl and asking the secret of her strength, as though he envied it. But at that moment, the natural situation was reversed. His eyes were lustreless, tired, without energy. Hers were suddenly bright and flashing with determination, and with the expression of her new-found will. Vjera felt that all at once a change had come over her, the weak strings of her heart grew strong, the dreamy hopelessness of her thoughts fell away, leaving one clearly defined resolution in its place. The man she loved was going mad, and she would save him, cost what it might.

That Faith, no larger than the tiniest mustard seed, but able to toss the mountains, as pebbles, from their foundations into the sea, is the determination to do the thing chosen to be done or to die—literally, to die—in the trying to do it. Death is farther from most of us than we fancy, and if we would but risk all, to win or lose all, we could almost always do the deed which looks so grimly impossible. Those who have faced great physical dangers, or who have been matched by fate against overwhelming odds of anxiety and trouble, alone know what great things are done when men stand at bay and face the world, and fate, and life, and death and misfortune, all banded together against them, and say in their hearts, "We will win this fight or die." Then, at that word, when it is spoken earnestly, in sincerity and truth, the iron will rises up and takes possession of the feeble body, the doubting soul shakes off its hesitating weakness, is drawn back upon itself like a strong bow bent double, is compressed and full of a terrible latent power, like the handful of deadly explosive which, buried in the bosom of the rock, will presently shake the mighty cliff to its roots, as no thunderbolt could shake it.

Vjera had made up her mind that she would save the man she loved from the destruction which was coming upon him. How he was to be saved, she knew not, but then and there, on the pavement of the commonplace Munich street, she made her stand and faced the odds, as bravely as ever soldier faced the enemy's triumphant charge, though she was only a forlorn little Polish shell-maker, without much health or strength, and having very little understanding of the danger beyond that which was given to her by her love.

She fixed her eyes upon the Count's face as though she would have him obey her.

"I will help you, and make everything right," she said. "But you must tell me what the trouble is."

"But how can you help me, child?" he asked, beginning to grow calmer under her clear gaze. "It is such a very complicated case," he continued, falling back gradually into his own natural manner. "You see, my friends have probably arrived by this train, and yet I cannot go home until I have set this other matter right with Fischelowitz. It is true, I have left a word written for them on my table, and perhaps they are there now, waiting for me, and if I went home I could have the money at once. But then—it may be too late before I get here again—"

"What money?" asked Vjera, anxious to get at the truth without delay.

"Oh, it is an absurd thing," he answered, growing nervous again. "Quite absurd—and yet, it is fifty marks—and until they come, I do not see what to do. Fifty marks—to-day it seems so much, and to-morrow it will seem so little!" He made a poor attempt to smile, but his voice trembled.

"But these fifty marks—what do you need them for to-night?" Vjera asked, not understanding at all. "Will not to-morrow do as well?"

"No, no!" he cried in renewed anxiety. "It must be to-night, now, this very hour. If I do not pay the money, I am ruined, Vjera, disgraced for ever. It is a debt of honour—you do not understand what that means, child, nor how terrible it is for a man not to pay before the day is over—ah, if it were not a debt of honour!—but there is no time to be lost. It is almost dark already. Go home, dear Vjera, go home. I cannot go with you to-night, for I must find this money. Good-night—and then to-morrow—I have not forgotten, and you must not forget—but there is no time now—good-night!"

He suddenly broke away from her side and began walking quickly in the opposite direction, his head bent down, his arms swinging by his side. She ran after him and again took his arm, and looked into his face.

"You must not go away like this," she said, so firmly and with so much authority that he stood still. "You have only half explained the trouble to me, but I can help you. A debt of honour, you say—what will happen if you do not pay it?"

"I must die," answered the Count. "I could never respect myself again."

"You have borrowed this money of Fischelowitz and promised to pay it to-day? Is that it? Tell me."

"No—I never borrowed it. No, no—it was that villain, last winter, who gave him the Gigerl—"

"And Fischelowitz expects you to pay that!" cried Vjera, indignantly. "It is impossible."

"When I took the Gigerl away last night I promised to bring the fifty marks by to-night. I gave my word, my word as a gentleman, Vjera, which I cannot break—my word, as a gentleman," he repeated with something of his old dignity.

"It is monstrous that Fischelowitz should have taken such a promise," said Vjera.

"That does not alter the obligation," answered the Count proudly. "Besides, I gave it of my own accord. I did not wait for him to ask it, after his wife accused me of being the means of his losing the money."

"Oh, how could she be so heartless!" Vjera exclaimed.

"What was the use of telling you? I did not mean to. Good-night, Vjera dear—I must be quick." He tried to leave her, but she held him fast.

"I will get you the money at once," she said desperately and without the least hesitation. He started, in the utmost astonishment, staring at her as though he fancied that she had lost her senses.

"You! Why, Vjera, how can you imagine that I would take it from you, or how do you think it would be possible for you to find it? You are mad, my dear child, quite mad!"

In spite of everything, the tears broke from her eyes at the words which meant so much to her and which seemed to mean so little to him. But she brushed them bravely away.

"You say you love me—you know that I love you. Do you trust me? Do you believe in me? And if you do, why then believe that I will do what I say. And as for taking the fifty marks from me—will not your friends be here to-night, as you say, and will you not be able to give it all back very soon? Only wait here—or no, go into the shop and talk to Fischelowitz—I will bring it to you in less than an hour, I promise you that I will—"

"But how? Oh, Vjera—I am in such trouble that I could almost bring myself to borrow it of you if you could lend it—I despise myself, but it is growing so late, and it will only be until to-morrow, only for a few hours perhaps. If you will wait to-night I may bring it to you before bedtime. But—are you sure, Vjera? Have you really got it? If I should wait here—and you should not find it—and my word should be broken—"

"For your word I give you mine. You shall have it in an hour." She tried to throw so much certainty into her tone as might persuade him, and she succeeded. "Where will you wait for me? In the shop?" she asked.

"No—not there. In the Café here—I am tired—I will sit down and drink a cup of coffee. I think I have a little money—enough for that." He smiled faintly as he felt in his pockets. Then his face fell. On the previous evening, when they had led him away from the eating-house, he had carelessly given all he had—a mark and two pennies—to pay for his supper, throwing it to the fat hostess without any reckoning, as he went out. "Never mind," he said, after the fruitless search. "I will wait outside."

But Vjera thrust a silver piece into his hand and was gone before he could protest. And in this way she took upon herself the burden of the Count's debt of honour.

CHAPTER X

Vjera turned her head when she had reached the corner of the street, and saw that the Count had disappeared. He had entered the Café, and had evidently accepted her assurance that she would bring the money without delay. So far, at least, she had been successful. Though by far the most difficult portion of the enterprise lay before her, she was convinced that if she could really produce the fifty marks, the approaching catastrophe of total madness would be averted. Her determination was still so strong that she never doubted the possibility of performing her promise. Without hesitation, she returned to the shop, in search of Johann Schmidt, to whose energies and kindness she instinctively turned for counsel and help. As she came to the door she saw that he was just bidding good-night to his employer. She waited a moment and met him on the pavement as he came out.

"I must have fifty marks in an hour, Herr Schmidt," she said, boldly. "If I do not get it, something dreadful will happen."

"Fifty marks!" exclaimed the Cossack in a tone of amazement. If she had said fifty millions, the shock to his financial sense could not have been more severe. "It is an enormous sum," he said, slowly, while she fixed her eyes upon him, waiting for his answer. "What is the matter, Vjera? Have you not been able to pay your rent this year, and has old Homolka threatened to turn you out?"

"Oh no! It is worse than that, far worse than that! If it were only myself—" she hesitated.

"What is it? Who is it? Perhaps it is not so serious as you think. Tell me all about it."

"There is very little time—only an hour. He is going mad—really mad, Herr Schmidt, because he has given his word of honour to pay Herr Fischelowitz that money this evening. I only calmed him, by promising to bring the money at once."

"You promised that?" exclaimed Schmidt. "It was a very wild promise—"

"I will keep it, and you must help me. We have an hour. If we do not succeed he will never be himself again."

"But fifty marks!" Schmidt could not recover from his astonishment. "Oh, Vjera!" he exclaimed at last, in the simplicity of his heart, "how you must love him!"

"I would do more than that—if I could," she answered. "But come, you will help me, will you not? I have a ten-mark piece and an old thaler put away at home. That makes thirteen, and two I have in my pocket, fifteen and—I am afraid that is all," she concluded after a slight hesitation.

"And five are twenty," said the Cossack, producing the six which he had, and taking one silver piece out of the number to be returned to his pocket. The children must not starve on the morrow.

"Oh, thank you, Herr Schmidt!" cried poor Vjera in a joyful voice as she eagerly took the proffered coins. "Twenty already! Why, twenty-five will be half, will it not? And I am sure that we can find the rest, then."

"There is Dumnoff," said Schmidt. "He probably has something, too."

"But I could not borrow of him—besides, if he knew it was for the Count—and he is so rough—he would not give it to us."

"We shall see," answered the other, who knew his man. "Wait a moment. He is still inside."

He re-entered the shop, where Fischelowitz and his wife were conversing under the gaslight.

"I tell you," Akulina was saying, "that it is high time you got rid of him. The new workman from Vilna will take his place, and it is positively ridiculous to be made to submit to this madman's humours, and impertinence. What sort of a man are you, Christian Gregorovitch, to let the fellow carry off your Gigerl, with his airy promise to pay you the money to-day?"

"The Gigerl was broken," observed the tobacconist.

"Oh, it could have been mended; and if it was really stolen, was that our business, I would like to know? Nobody would ever have supposed, seeing it in our window, that it had been stolen. And it could have been mended, as I say, and might have been worth something after all. You never really tried to sell it, as you ought to have done from the very first. And now you have got nothing at all, nothing but that insolent maniac's promise. If I were you I would take the money out of his wages, I would indeed!"

"No doubt you would," said Fischelowitz, with sincere conviction.

Meanwhile Schmidt had gone into the back shop, where Dumnoff was still doggedly working, making up for the time he had lost by coming late in the morning. He was alone at his little table.

"How much money have you got?" asked the Cossack, briefly. Dumnoff looked up rather stupidly, dropped the cigarette he was making, and felt in his pocket for his change. He produced five marks, an unusual sum for him to have in his possession, and which would not have found itself in his hands had not his arrest on the previous evening prevented his spending considerably more than he had spent in his favourite corn-brandy.

"I want it all," said Schmidt.

"You are a cool-blooded fellow," laughed Dumnoff, making as though he would return the coins to his pocket.

"Look here, Dumnoff," answered the Cossack, his bright eyes gleaming. "I want that money. You know me, and you had better give it to me without making any trouble."

Dumnoff seemed confused by the sharpness of the demand, and hesitated.

"You seem in a great hurry," he said, with an awkward laugh, "I suppose you mean to give it back to me?"

"You shall have it at the rate of a mark a day in the next five work days. You will get your pay this evening and that will be quite enough for you to get drunk with to-night."

"That is true," said Dumnoff, thoughtfully. "Well, take it," he added, slipping the money into the other's outstretched palm.

"Thank you," said the Cossack. "You are not so bad as you look, Dumnoff. Good-night." He was gone in a moment.

Dumnoff stared at the door through which he had disappeared.

"After all," he muttered, discontentedly, "he could not have taken it by force. I wonder why I was such a fool as to give it to him!"

"I tell you," said Akulina to her husband as Schmidt passed through the outer shop, "that he will end by costing us so much in money lent, and squandered in charity, that the business will go to dust and feathers! I am only a weak woman, Christian Gregorovitch, but I have four children—"

The Cossack heard no more, for he closed the street door behind him and returned to Vjera's side. She was standing as he had left her, absorbed in the contemplation of the financial crisis.

"Five more," said he, giving her the silver. "That is one half. Now for the other. But are you quite sure, Vjera, that it is as bad as you think? I know that Fischelowitz does not in the least expect the money."

"No—I daresay not. But I know this, if I had not met him just now and promised to bring him the fifty marks, he would have been raving mad before morning." Schmidt saw by her look that she was convinced of the fact.

"Very well," he said. "I am not going to turn back now. The poor Count has done me many a good turn in his time, and I will do my best, though I do not exactly see what more I can do, at such short notice."

"Have you got anything worth pawning, Herr Schmidt?" asked Vjera, ruthless, as devoted people can be when the object of their devotion is in danger.

"Well—I have not much that I can spare. There is the bed—but my wife cannot sleep on the floor, though I would myself. And there are a few pots and pans in the kitchen—not worth much, and I do not know what we should do without them. I do not know, I am sure. I cannot take the children's things, Vjera, even for you."

"No," said Vjera doubtfully. "I suppose not. Of course not!" she exclaimed, immediately afterwards, with an attempt to express conviction.

"There is one thing—there is the old samovar," continued the Cossack. "It has a leak in one side, and we make the tea as we can, when we have any. But I remember that I once pawned it, years ago, for five marks."

"That would make thirty," said Vjera promptly.

"I do not believe they would lend so much on it now, though it is good metal. It is a little battered, besides being leaky."

"Let us get it," said Vjera, beginning to walk briskly on. "I have something, too, though I do not know what it is worth. It is an old skin of a wolf—my father killed it inside the village, just before we came away."

"A wolf skin!" exclaimed Schmidt. "That may be worth something, if it is good."

"I am afraid it is not very good," answered Vjera doubtfully. "The hair comes out. I think it must have been a mangy wolf. And there is a bad hole on one side."

"It was probably badly cured," said the Cossack, who understood furs. "But I can mend the hole in five minutes, so that nobody will see it."

"We will get it, too. But I am afraid that it will not be nearly enough to make up the twenty-five marks. They could not possibly give us twenty marks for the skin, could they?"

"No, indeed, unless you could sell it to some one who does not understand those things. And the samovar will not bring five, as I said. We must find something else."

"Let us get the samovar first," said Vjera decisively. "I will wait downstairs till you get it, and then you will wait for me where I live, and after that we will go together. I may find something else. Indeed, I must, or we shall not have enough."

They walked rapidly through the deepening shadows towards Schmidt's home. Vjera moved, as people do, who are possessed by an idea which must be put into immediate execution, her head high, her eyes full of light, her lips set, her step firm. Her companion was surprised to find that he needed to walk fast in order to keep by her side. He looked at her often, as he had looked all day, with an expression that showed at once much interest, considerable admiration and some pity. If he had not been lately brought to some new opinion concerning the girl he would certainly not have entered into her wild scheme for calming the Count's excitement without at least arguing the case lengthily, and discussing all the difficulties which presented themselves to his imagination. As it was, he felt himself carried away by a sort of enthusiasm in her cause, which would have led him to make even greater sacrifices than he had it in his power to offer. So strong was this feeling that he felt called upon to make a sort of apology.

"I am sorry I cannot do more to help you," he said regretfully. "It is very little I know, but then, you see I am not alone in the world, Vjera. There are others to be thought of. And besides, I have just paid the rent, and there are no savings left."

"Dear Herr Schmidt," answered Vjera gratefully, "you are doing too much already—but I cannot help taking all you give me, though I can thank you for it with all my heart."

They did not speak again during the next few minutes, until they reached the door of the house in which the Cossack lived.

"I shall only need a moment," he said, as he dived into the dark entrance.

He lost so little time, that it seemed to Vjera as though the echo of his steps had not died away upon the stairs before she heard his footfall again as he descended. This time, however, there was a rattle and clatter of metal to be heard as well as his quick tread and the loud creaking of his coarse, stiff shoes. He emerged into the street with the body of the samovar under one arm. The movable brass chimney of the machine was sticking out of one of his pockets, and in his left hand he had its little tray, with the rings and other pieces belonging to the whole. Amongst those latter objects, which he grasped tightly in his fingers, there figured also the fragment of a small spoon of which the bowl had been broken from the handle.

"It is silver," he said, referring to the latter utensil, as he held up the whole handful before Vjera's eyes. "But if we can find a jeweller's shop open, we will sell it. We can get more for it in that way. And now your wolf's skin, Vjera. And be sure to bring me a needle and some strong thread when you come down. I can mend the hole by the gaslight in the street, for Homolka would not understand it if he saw me going to your room, you know."

She helped him to put all the smaller things into his pockets, so that he had only the samovar itself, and its metal tray to carry in his hands, and then they went briskly on towards Vjera's lodging.

"Do you think we shall get three marks for the little spoon?" she asked, constantly preoccupied by her calculations.

"Oh yes," Schmidt answered cheerfully. "We may get five. It is good silver, and they buy silver by weight."

A few moments later she stood still before a narrow shop which was lighted within, though there was no lamp in the windows. It was that of a small watchmaker and jeweller, and a few silver watches and some cheap chains and trinkets were visible behind the glass pane.

"Perhaps he may buy the spoon," suggested Vjera, anxious to lose no time.

Without a word Schmidt entered the shop, while the girl stood outside. In less than five minutes he came out again with something in his hand.

"Three and a half," he said, handing her the money.

"I had hoped it would be worth more," she answered, putting the coins with the rest.

"No. He weighed it with silver marks. It weighed just four of them, and he said he must have half a mark to make it worth his while."

"Very well," said Vjera, "it is always something. I have twenty-eight and a half now."

When they reached her lodging Schmidt set down the samovar upon the pavement and made himself a cigarette, while he waited for her. She was gone a long time, as it seemed to him, and he was beginning to wonder whether anything had happened, when she suddenly made her appearance, noiseless in her walk, as always. The old wolf's skin was hung over one shoulder, and she carried besides a limp-looking brown paper parcel, tied with a bit of folded ribband. As he caught sight of her face in the light of the street lamp, Schmidt fancied that she was paler than before, and that her cheek was wet.

"I am sorry I was so long," she said. "The little sister cried because I would not stay, and I had to quiet her. Here is the skin. Do you see? I am afraid this is a very big hole—and the hair comes out in handfuls. Look at it."

"It was a very old wolf," remarked the Cossack, holding the skin up under the gaslight.

"Does that make it worth less?" asked Vjera anxiously.

"Not of itself; on the contrary. And I can mend the hole, if you have the thread and needle. The worst thing about it all is the way the hairs fall out. I am afraid the moths have been at it, Vjera." He shook his head gravely. "I am afraid the moths have done a great deal of damage."

"Oh, if I had only known—I would have been so careful! And to think that it might have been worth something."

"It is worth something as it is, but at the pawnbroker's they will not lend much on it." He took the threaded needle, which she had not forgotten, and sitting down upon the edge of the pavement spread the skin upon his knees with the fur downwards. Then he quickly began to draw the hole together, sewing it firmly with the furrier's cross stitch, and so neatly that the seam looked like a single straight line on the side of the leather, while it was quite invisible in the fur on the other.

"What is the other thing you have brought?" he inquired without looking up from his work. The light was bad, and he had to bend his eyes close to the sewing.

"It is something I may be able to sell," said Vjera in a rather unsteady voice.

"Silver?" asked Schmidt, cheerfully.

"Oh no—not silver—something dearer," she said, almost under her breath. "I am afraid it is very hard for you to see," she added quickly, attempting to avoid his questions. "Do you not think that I could hold a match for you, to make a little more light? You always have some with you."

"Wait a moment—yes—I have almost finished the seam—here is the box. Now, if you can hold the match just there, just over the needle, and keep it from going out, I can finish the end off neatly."

Vjera knelt down beside him and held the flickering bit of wood as well as she was able. They made a strange picture, out in the unfrequented street, the dim glare of the gaslight above them, and the redder flame of the match making odd tints and shadows in their faces. Vjera's shawl had slipped back from her head and her thick tress of red-brown hair had found its way over her shoulder. An artist, strolling supperwards from his studio, came down their side of the way. He stopped and looked at them.

"Has anything happened?" he asked kindly. "Can I be of any use?"

Vjera looked up with a frightened glance. The Cossack paid no attention to the stranger.

"Oh no, thank you—thank you, sir, it is nothing—only a little piece of work to finish."

The artist gave one more look and passed on, wishing that he could have had pencil and paper and light at his command for five minutes.

"There," said Schmidt triumphantly. "It is done, and very well done. And now for the pawn-shop, Vjera!"

Vjera took the skin over her arm and her companion picked up the samovar with its tray, and they moved on again. Vjera's face was pale and sad, but she seemed more confident of success than ever, and her step was elastic and hopeful. Johann Schmidt's curiosity was very great, as has been seen on previous occasions. He did his best to control it, for some time, only trying to guess from the general appearance of the limp parcel what it might contain. But his ingenuity failed to solve the problem. At last he could bear it no longer. They were entering the street where the pawnbroker's shop was situated when his resolution broke down.

"Is it a piece of lace?" he asked at a venture. "If it is, you know, and if it is good, it may be worth all the other things together."

"No. It is not a piece of lace," answered the girl. "I will tell you what it is, if we do not get enough without it."

"I only thought," explained the Cossack, "that if we were going to try and pawn it, I had better know—"

"We cannot pawn it," said Vjera decisively. "It will have to be sold. Let us go in together." She spoke the last words as they reached the door of the pawn-shop.

"I could save you the trouble," Schmidt suggested, offering to take the wolf's skin. But Vjera would not give it up. She felt that she must see everything done herself, if only to distract her thoughts from more painful matters.

The place was half full of people, most of them with anxious faces, and all having some object or other in their hands. The pawn-shops do their best business in the evening. A man and a woman, both advanced in middle age, well fed, parsimoniously washed and possessing profiles of an outline disquieting to Christian prejudices, leaned over the counter, handled the articles offered them, consulted each other in incomprehensible monosyllables, talked volubly to the customers in oily undertones and from time to time counted out small doses of change which they gave to the eager recipients, accompanied by little slips of paper on which there were both printed and written words. The room was warm and redolent of poverty. A broad flame of gas burned, without a shade, over the middle of the counter.

In spite of their unctuous tones the Hebrew and his wife did their business rapidly, with sharpness and decision. Either one of them would have undertaken to name the precise pawning value of anything on earth and, possibly, of most things in heaven, provided that the universe were brought piecemeal to their counter. Both Vjera and Schmidt had been made acquainted by previous necessities with the establishment. Vjera held her paper parcel in her hand. The other things were laid together upon the counter. The Hebrew woman glanced at the samovar, felt the weight of it and turned it once round.

"Leaky," she observed in her smooth voice. "Old brass. One mark and a half." Her husband put out his hand, touched the machine, lifted it, and nodded.

"Only a mark and a half!" exclaimed Vjera. "And the skin, how much for that?"

"It is a genuine Russian wolf," Schmidt put in. "And it is very large."

"Moth-eaten," said the Jewess. "And there is a hole in the side. Five marks."

Schmidt held the fur up to the light and blew into it with a professional air, as furriers do.

"Look at that!" he cried, persuasively. "Why, it is worth twenty!"

The Hebrew lady, instead of answering extended a fat thumb and a plump, pointed forefinger, and pinching a score of hairs between the two, pulled them out without effort, and then held them close to the Cossack's eyes.

"Five marks," she repeated, getting the money out and preparing to fill in a couple of pawn-tickets.

"Make it ten, with the samovar!" entreated Vjera. The Jewess smiled.

"Do you think the samovar is of gold?" she inquired. "Six and a half for the two. Take it or leave it."

Vjera looked at Schmidt anxiously as though to ask his opinion.

"They will not give more," he said, in Russian.

The girl took the money and the flimsy tickets and they went out into the street. Vjera hesitated as to the direction she should take, and Schmidt looked to her as though awaiting her orders.

"Twenty-eight and a half and six and a half are thirty-five," she said, thoughtfully. "And we have nothing more to give, but this. I must sell it, Herr Schmidt."

"Well, what is it?" he asked, glad to know the secret at last.

"It is my mother's hair. She cut it off herself when she knew she was dying and she told me to sell it if ever I needed a little money."

The girl's voice trembled violently, and she turned her head away. Schmidt was silent and very grave. Then Vjera began to move on again, clutching the precious thing to her bosom and drawing her shawl over it.

"The best man for this lives in the Maffei Strasse," said Schmidt after a few minutes.

"Show me the way." Vjera turned as he directed. At that moment she would have lost herself in the familiar streets, had he not been there to guide her.

The hairdresser's shop was brilliantly lighted, and as good fortune would have it, there were no customers within. With an entreating glance which he obeyed, Vjera made Schmidt wait outside.

"Please do not look!" she whispered. "I can bear it better alone." The good fellow nodded and began to walk up and down.

As Vjera entered the shop, the chief barber in command waltzed forward, as hairdressers always seem to waltz. At the sight of the poor girl, however, he assumed a stern appearance which, to tell the truth, was out of character with his style of beauty. His rich brown locks were curled and anointed in a way that might have aroused envy in the heart of an Assyrian dandy in the palmy days of Sardanapalus.

"Do you buy hair?" asked Vjera, timidly offering her limp parcel.

"Oh, certainly, sometimes," answered the barber. The youth in attendance—the barber tadpole of the hairdresser frog—abandoned the cleansing of a comb and came forward with a leer, in the hope that Vjera might turn out to be pretty on a closer inspection. In this he was disappointed.

The man took the parcel and laid it on one of the narrow marble tables placed before a mirror in a richly gilt frame. He pushed aside the blue glass powder-box, the vial of brilliantine and the brushes. Vjera untied the bit of faded ribband herself and opened the package. The contents exhaled a faint, sickly odour.

A tress of beautiful hair, of unusual length and thickness, lay in the paper. The colour was that which is now so much sought after, and which great ladies endeavour to produce upon their own hair, when they have any, by washing it with extra-dry champagne, while little ladies imitate them with a humble solution of soda. The colour in question is a reddish-brown with rich golden lights in it, and it is very rare in nature.

The barber eyed the thick plait with a businesslike expression.

"The colour is not so bad," he remarked, as though suggesting that it might have been very much better.

"Surely, it is very beautiful hair!" said Vjera, her heart almost breaking at the sight of the tenderly treasured heirloom.

Suddenly the man snuffed the odour, lifted the tress to his nose, and smelt it. Then he laid it down again and took the thicker end, which was tied tightly with a ribband, in his hands, pulling at the short lengths of hair which projected beyond the knot. They broke very easily, with an odd, soft snap.

"It is worth nothing at all," said the barber decisively. "It is a pity, for it is a very pretty colour."

Vjera started, and steadied herself against the back of the professional chair which stood by the table.

"Nothing?" she repeated, half stupid with the pain of her disappointment. "Nothing? not even fifteen marks?"

"Nothing. It is rotten, and could not be worked. The hairs break like glass."

Vjera pressed her left hand to her side as though something hurt her. The tadpole youth grinned idiotically and the barber seemed anxious to end the interview.

With a look of broken-hearted despair the girl turned to the table and began to do up her parcel again. Her shawl fell to the ground as she moved. Then the tadpole nudged his employer and pointed at Vjera's long, red-brown braid, and grinned again from ear to ear.

"Is it fifteen marks that you want?" asked the man.

"Fifteen—yes—I must have fifteen," repeated Vjera in dull tones.

"I will give it to you for your own hair," said the barber with a short laugh.

"For my own?" cried Vjera, suddenly turning round. It had never occurred to her that her own tress could be worth anything. "For my own?" she repeated as though not believing her ears.

"Yes—let me see," said the man. "Turn your head again, please. Let me see. Yes, yes, it is good hair of the kind, though it has not the gold lights in it that the other had. But, to oblige you, I will give you fifteen for it."

"But I must have the money now," said Vjera, suspiciously. "You must give me the money now, to take with me. I cannot wait."

The barber smiled, and produced a gold piece and five silver ones.

"You may hold the money in your hand," he said, offering it to her, "while you sit down and I do the work."

Vjera clutched the coins fiercely and placed herself in the big chair before the mirror. She could see in the glass that her eyes were on fire. The barber loosened a screw in the back of the seat and removed the block with the cushion, handing it to his assistant.

"The scissors, and a comb, Anton," he said briskly, lifting at the same time the heavy tress and judging its weight. The reflection of the steel flashed in the mirror, as the artist quickly opened and shut the scissors, with that peculiar shuffling jingle which only barbers can produce.

"Wait a minute!" cried Vjera, with sudden anxiety, and turning her head as though to draw away her hair from his grasp. "One minute—please—fifteen and thirty-five are really fifty, are they not?"

The tadpole began to count on his fingers, whispering audibly.

"Yes," answered the barber. "Fifteen and thirty-five are fifty."

The tadpole desisted, having already got into mathematical difficulties in counting from one hand over to the other.

"Then cut it off quickly, please!" said poor Vjera, settling herself in the chair again, and giving her head to the shears.

In the silence that followed, only the soft jingle of the scissors was heard.

"There!" exclaimed the hairdresser, holding up a hand-mirror behind her. "I have been generous, you see. I have not cut it very short. See for yourself."

"Thank you," said Vjera. "You are very kind." She saw nothing, indeed, but she was satisfied, and rose quickly.

She tied up the limp parcel with the same old piece of faded ribband, and a little colour suddenly came into her face as she pressed it to her bosom. All at once, she lost control of herself, and with a sharp sob the tears gushed out. She stooped a little and drew her shawl over her head to hide her face. The tears wet her hands and the brown paper, and fell down to the greasy marble floor of the shop.

"It will grow again very soon," said the barber, not unkindly. He supposed, naturally enough, that she was weeping over her sacrifice.

"Oh no! It is not that!" she cried. "I am so—so happy to have kept this!" Then, without another word, she slipped noiselessly out into the street, clasping the precious relic to her breast.

CHAPTER XI

"I have got it—I have got it all!" cried Vjera, as she came up with Schmidt on the pavement. His quick eye caught sight of the parcel, only half hidden by her shawl.

"But you have brought the hair away with you," he said, in some anxiety, and fearing a mistake or some new trouble.

"Yes," she answered. "That is the best of it." Her tears had disappeared as suddenly as they had come, and she could now hardly restrain the nervous laughter that rose to her lips.

"But how is that?" asked Schmidt, stopping.

"I gave them my own," she laughed, hysterically. "I gave them my own—instead. Quick, quick—there is no time to lose. Is it an hour yet, since I left him?" She ran along, and Schmidt found it hard to keep beside her without running, too. At last he broke into a sort of jog-trot. In five minutes they were at the door of the café.

The Count was sitting at a small table near the door, an empty coffee-cup before him, staring with a fixed look at the opposite wall. There were few people in the place, as the performances at the theatres had already begun. Vjera entered alone.

"I have brought you the money," she said, joyfully, as she stood beside him and laid a hand upon his arm to attract his attention, for he had not noticed her coming.

"The money?" he said, excitedly. "The fifty marks? You have got it?"

She sat down at the table, and began to count the gold and silver, producing it from her pocket in instalments of four or five coins, and making little heaps of them before him.

"It is all there—every penny of it," she said, counting the piles again.

The poor man's eyes seemed starting from his head, as he leaned eagerly forward over the money.

"Is it real? Is it true?" he asked in a low voice. "Oh, Vjera, do not laugh at me—is it really true, child?"

"Really true—fifty marks." Her pale face beamed with pleasure. "And now you can go and pay Fischelowitz at once," she added.

But he leaned back a moment in his chair, looking at her intently. Then his eyes grew moist, and, when he spoke, his voice quivered.

"May God forgive me for taking it of you," he said. "You have saved me, Vjera—saved my honour, my life—all. God bless you, dear, God bless you! I am very, very thankful."

He put the coins carefully together and wrapped them in his silk handkerchief, and rose from his seat. He had already paid for his cup of coffee. They went out together. The Cossack had disappeared.

"You have saved my life and my honour—my honour and my life," repeated the Count, softly and dwelling on the words in a dreamy way.

"I will wait outside," said Vjera as they reached the tobacconist's shop, a few seconds later.

The Count turned to her and laid both hands upon her shoulders, looking into her face.

"You cannot understand what you have done for me," he said earnestly.

He stooped, for he was much taller than she, and closing his tired eyes for a moment, he pressed his lips upon her waxen forehead. Before he had seen the bright blush that glowed in her cheeks, he had entered the shop.

Akulina was seated in one corner, apparently in a bad humour, for her dark face was flushed, and her small eyes looked up savagely at the Count. Her husband was leaning over the counter, smoking and making a series of impressions in violet ink upon the back of an old letter, with an india-rubber stamp in which the word "Celebrated Manufactory" held a prominent place. He nodded familiarly.

"Herr Fischelowitz," said the Count, regaining suddenly his dignity of manner and bearing, "in the course of the conversation last evening, I said that I would to-day refund the fifty marks which you once lent to that atrocious young man who wore green glasses. I daresay you remember the circumstance?"

"I had quite forgotten it," said Fischelowitz. "Please do not allow it to trouble you, my dear Count. I never considered you responsible for it, and of course you cannot—"

"It is a shame!" Akulina broke in, angrily. "You ought to make him pay it out of what he earns, since he took the Gigerl!"

"Madam," said the Count, addressing her with great civility, "if it is agreeable to you, we will not discuss the matter. I only reminded Herr Fischelowitz of what took place because—"

"Because you have no money—of course!" interrupted Akulina.

"On the contrary, because I have brought the money, and shall be obliged to you if you will count it."

Akulina's jaw dropped, and Fischelowitz looked up in amazement. The Count produced his knotted handkerchief and laid it on the table.

"I only wish you to understand," he said, speaking to Akulina, "that when a gentleman gives his word he keeps it. Will you do me the favour to count the money?"

"Of course, it is no business of ours to find out how he got it," observed Akulina, rising and coming forward.

"None whatever, madam," answered the Count, spreading out the coins which had been collected by loving hands from so many sources. "The only question is, to ascertain whether there are fifty marks here or not."

Fischelowitz stood looking on. He had not yet recovered from his surprise, and was half afraid that there might be something wrong. But the practical Akulina lost no time in assuring herself that the sum was complete. As she realised this fact, her features relaxed into a pleasant smile.

"Well, Count," she said, "we are very much obliged to you for this. It is very honest of you, for of course, you were not exactly called upon—"

"I understood you to say that I was," replied the Count, gravely.

"Oh, that was yesterday, and I am very sorry if I annoyed you. But let bygones be bygones! I hope there is no ill-will between us?"

"Oh, none at all," returned the other indifferently. "I have the honour to wish you a very good evening." Without waiting for more, the Count bowed and left the shop.

"Akulina," said Fischelowitz, thoughtfully, as the door closed, "that man is a gentleman, say what you please."

"A pretty gentleman," laughed Akulina, putting the money into the till. "A gentleman indeed—why, look at his coat!"

"And you are a fool, Akulina," added Fischelowitz, handling his india-rubber stamp.

"Thank you; but for my foolery you would be fifty marks poorer to-night, Christian Gregorovitch. A gentleman, pah!"

The Count had drawn Vjera's willing arm through his, and they were walking slowly away together.

"I must be going home," she said, reluctantly. "The little sister will be crying for me. I cannot leave her any longer."

"Not till I have thanked you, dear," he answered, pressing her arm to his side. "But I will go with you to your door, and thank you all the way—though the way is far too short for all I have to say."

"I have done nothing—it has really cost me nothing." Vjera squeezed her limp parcel under her shawl, and felt that she was speaking the truth.

"I cannot believe that, Vjera," said the Count. "You could not have found so much money so quickly, without making some great sacrifice. But I will give it back to you—"

"Oh no—no," she cried, earnestly. "Make no promises to me. Think what this promise has cost you. When you have the money, you may give it back if you choose—but it would make me so unhappy if you promised."

"Would it, child? And yet, my friends are waiting for me, and they have money for me, too. Then, I will only say that I will give it back to you as soon as possible. Is that right?"

"Yes—and nothing more than that. And as for thanking me—what have I done that needs thanks? Would you not have done as much for me if—if, for instance, I had been ill, and could not pay the rent of the room? And then—think of the happiness I have had!"

The words were spoken so simply and it was so clear that they were true, that the Count found it hard to answer. Not because he had nothing to express, but because the words for the expression could not be found. Again he pressed her arm.

"Vjera," he said, when they had walked some distance farther, "it is of no use to speak of this. There is that between you and me which makes speech contemptible and words ridiculous. There is only one thing that I can do, Vjera dearest. I can love you, dear, with all my heart. Will you take my love for thanks—and my devotion for gratitude? Will you, dear? Will you remember what you promised and what I promised last night? As soon as all is right, to-morrow, will you be my wife?"

"If it could ever be!" sighed the poor girl, recalled suddenly to the remembrance of his pitiful infirmity.

"It can be, it shall be and it will be," he answered in tones of conviction. "They are waiting for me now, Vjera, in my little room—but they may wait, for I will not lose a moment of your dear company for them all. They are waiting for me with the money and the papers and the orders. I have waited long for them, they can afford to have a little patience now. And to-morrow, at this time, we shall be together, Vjera, in the train—I will have a special carriage for you and me, and then, a night and a day and another night and we shall be at home—for ever. How happy we shall be! Will you not be happy with me, darling? Why do you sigh?"

"Did I sigh?" asked Vjera, trying to laugh a little.

He hardly noticed the question, but began to talk again, as he had talked on the previous evening, describing all that he meant to do, and all that they would do together. Vjera heard and tried not to listen. Her joy was all gone. The great, overwhelming pleasure she had felt in dispelling his anxiety and in averting what had seemed a near and terrible catastrophe, gave place to the old, heartrending pity for him, as he rambled on in his delusion. She had hoped that, as it was late on Wednesday evening, the time of it was passed and that, for another week, he would talk no more of his friends and his money and his return to fortune. But the fixed idea was there still, as dominant as ever. Her light tread grew weary and her head sank forward as she walked. For one short hour she had felt the glory of sacrificing all she had to give, to her love. Are there many who have felt as much, with as good reason, in a whole lifetime?

But the hour was gone, taking with it the reality and leaving in its place a memory, fair, brilliant, and dear as the tress of golden hair Vjera was carrying home in her parcel, but as useless perhaps and as valueless in the world of realities as that had proved to be.

They reached her door and stopped in their walk. She looked up sadly into his eyes, as she held out her hand. He hesitated a moment, and then threw both his arms round her and drew her to his heart and kissed her passionately again and again. She tried to draw back.

"Oh no, no!" she cried. "It cannot be so to-morrow—why should you kiss me to-day?" But he would not let her go. She loved him, though she knew he was mad, and she let her head fall upon his shoulder, and allowed herself to believe in love for a moment.

Suddenly she felt that he was startled by something.

"Vjera!" he cried. "Have you cut off your beautiful hair? What have you done, child? How could you do it?"

"It was so heavy," she said, looking up with a bright smile. "It made my head ache—it is best so."

But he was not satisfied, for he guessed something of the truth, and the pain and horror that thrilled him told him that he had guessed rightly.

"You have cut it off—and you have sold it—you have sold your hair for me—" he stammered in a broken voice.

She hung her head a little.

"I always meant to cut it off. I did not care for it, you know. And besides," she added, suddenly looking up again, "you will not love me less, will you? They said it would grow again—you will not love me less?"

"Love you less? Ah, Vjera, that promise I may make at least—never—to the end of ends!"

"And yet," she answered, "if it should all be true—if it only should—you could not—oh, I should not be worthy of you—you could never marry me."

The Count drew back a step and held out his right hand, with a strangely earnest look in his weary eyes. She laid her fingers in his almost unconsciously. Then, as though he were in a holy place, he took off his hat, and stood bareheaded before her.

"If I forsake you, Vjera," he said very solemnly, "if I forsake you ever, in riches or in poverty, in honour or in disrepute, may the God of heaven forsake me in the hour of my death."

He swore the great oath deliberately, in a strong, clear voice, and then was silent for a moment, his eyes turned upwards, his attitude unchanged. Then he raised the poor girl's thin hand to his lips and kissed it, three times, reverently, as devout persons kiss the relics of departed saints.

"Good-night, Vjera," he said, quietly. "We shall meet to-morrow."

Vjera was awed by his solemn earnestness, and strongly moved by his action.

"Good-night," she answered, lovingly. "Heaven bless you and keep you safe." She looked for a last time into his face, as though trying to impress upon her mind the memories of that fateful evening, and then she withdrew into the house, shutting the street door behind her.

The Count stood still for several minutes, unconsciously holding his hat in his hand. At last he covered his head and walked slowly away in the direction of his home. By degrees his mind fell into its old groove and he hastened his steps. From time to time, he fancied that some one was following him at no great distance, but though he glanced quickly over his shoulder he saw no one in the dimly-lighted street. The door of the house in which he lived was open, and he ran up the stairs at a great pace, sure that by this time his friends must be waiting for him in his room. When he reached it, all was dark and quiet. The echo of his own footsteps seemed still to resound in the staircase as he closed his door and struck a match. He found his small lamp in a corner, lighted it with some difficulty, set it on the table and sat down. There, beside him, propped up against two books, was the piece of paper on which he had written the few words for his friends, in case they came while he was out. He took it up, looked over it absently and began to fold it upon itself again and again.

"Dear Vjera!" he exclaimed, in a low caressing tone, as he smoothed the folded strip between his fingers.

He was thinking, and thinking connectedly, of all that had just taken place, and wondering how it was that he had been able to accept such a sacrifice from one so little able to sacrifice anything. It seemed as though it should have been impossible for him to let the poor little shell-maker take upon herself his burden, and free him of it and set him right again in his own eyes.

"I know that I love her now," he said to himself.

And he was right. There are secret humiliations to which no man would submit, as such, but from which love, when it is real, can take away the sting and the poison. The man of heart, who does not love but is loved in spite of himself, fears to accept a sacrifice, lest in so doing he should seem to declare his readiness to do as he is done by, from like motives. But when love is on both sides there is no such drawing back from love's responsibilities. The sacrifice is accepted not only with gratitude, but with joy, as a debt of which the repayment by sacrifice again constitutes in itself a happiness. And thus, perhaps, it is that they love best who love in sorrow and in want, in worldly poverty and in distress of soul, for they alone can know what joy it is to receive, and what yet infinitely greater joy lies in giving all when all is sorely needed.

But as the Count dwelt on the circumstances he saw also what it was that Vjera had done, and he wondered how she could have found the strength to do it. He did not, indeed, say to himself that for his sake she had parted with her only beauty, for he had never considered whether she were good-looking or not. The bond between them was of a different nature, and would not have been less strong had Vjera been absolutely ugly instead of being merely, what is called, plain. He would have loved her as well, had she been a cripple, or deformed, just as she loved him in spite of his madness. But he knew well enough how women, even the most wretched, value their hair when it is beautiful, what care they bestow upon it and what consolation they derive from the rich, silken coil denied to fairer women than themselves. There is something in the thought of cutting off the heavy tress and selling it which appeals to the pity of most people, and which, to women themselves, is full of horror. A man might have felt the same in those days when long locks were the distinctive outward sign of nobility in man, and perhaps the respect of that obsolete custom has left in the minds of most people a sort of unconscious tradition. However that may be, we all feel that in one direction, at least, a woman's sacrifice can go no further than in giving her head to the shears.

The longer the Count thought of this, the more his gratitude increased, and the more fully he realised at what great cost poor Vjera had saved him from what he considered the greatest conceivable dishonour, from the shame of breaking his word, no matter under what conditions it had been given. He could, of course, repay her the money, so soon as his friends arrived, but by no miracle whatever could he restore to her head the only beauty it had ever possessed. He had scarcely understood this at first, for he had been confused and shaken by the many emotions which had in succession played upon his nervous mind and body during the past twenty-four hours. But now he saw it all very clearly. He had taken only money, which he would be able to restore; she had given a part of herself, irrevocably.

So deeply absorbed was he in his thoughts that the clocks struck many successive quarters without rousing him from his reverie, or suggesting again to him the fixed idea by which his life was governed on that day of the week. But as midnight drew near, the prolonged striking of the bells at every quarter at last attracted his attention. He started suddenly and rose from his seat, trying to count the strokes, but he had not heard the first ones and was astray in his reckoning. It was very late, that was certain, and not many minutes could elapse before the door would open and his friends would enter. He hastily smoothed his hair, looked to the flame of his bright little lamp and made a trip of inspection round the room. Everything was in order. He was almost glad that they were to come at night, for the lamplight seemed to lend a more cheerful look to the room. The Turkey-red cotton counterpane on the bed looked particularly well, the Count thought. During the next fifteen minutes he walked about, rubbing his hands softly together. At the first stroke of the following quarter he stood still and listened intently.

Four quarters struck, and then the big bell began to toll the hour. It must be eleven, he thought, as he counted the strokes. Eleven—twelve—he started, and turned very white, but listened still, for he knew that he should hear another clock striking in a few seconds. As the strokes followed each other, his heart beat like a fulling-hammer, giving a succession of quick blows, and pausing to repeat the rhythmic tattoo more loudly and painfully than before. Ten—eleven—twelve—there was no mistake. The day was over. It was midnight, and no one had come. The room swam with him.

Then, as in a vision of horror, he saw himself standing there, as he had stood many times before, listening for the last stroke, and suddenly awaking from the dream to the crushing disappointment of the reality. For one brief and terrible moment his whole memory was restored to him and he knew that his madness was only madness, and nothing more, and that it seized him in the same way, week by week, through the months and the years, leaving him thus on the stroke of twelve each Wednesday night, a broken, miserable, self-deceived man. As in certain dreams, we dream that we have dreamed the same things before, so with him an endless calendar of Wednesdays was unrolled before his inner sight, all alike, all ending in the same terror of conscious madness.

He had dreamed it all, there was no one to come to him in his distress, no one would ever enter that lonely room to bring back to him the treasures of a glorious past, for there was no one to come. It had all been a dream from beginning to end and there was no reality in it.

He staggered to his chair and sat down, pressing his lean hands to his aching temples and rocking himself to and fro, his breath hissing through his convulsively closed teeth. Still the fearful memory remained, and it grew into a prophetic vision of the future, reflecting what had been upon the distant scenery of what was yet to be. With that one deadly stroke of the great church bell, all was gone—fortune, friends, wealth, dignity. The majestic front of the palace of his hopes was but a flimsy, painted tissue. The fire that ran through his tortured brain consumed the gaudy, artificial thing in the flash and rush of a single flame, and left behind only the charred skeleton framework, which had supported the vast canvas. And then, he saw it again and again looming suddenly out of the darkness, brightening into beauty and the semblance of strength, to be as suddenly destroyed once more. With each frantic beat of his heart the awful transformation was renewed. For dreams need not time to spin out their intolerable length. With each burning throb of his raging blood, every nerve in his body, every aching recess of his brain, was pierced and twisted, and pierced again with unceasing agony.

Then a new horror was added to the rest. He saw before him the poor Polish girl, her only beauty shorn away for his sake, he saw all that he had promised in return, and he knew that he had nothing to give her, nothing, absolutely, save the crazy love of a wretched madman. He could not even repay her the miserable money which had cost her so dear. Out of his dreams of fortune there was not so much as a handful of coin left to give the girl who had given all she had, who had sold her hair to save his honour. With frightful vividness the truth came over him. That honour of his, he had pledged it in the recklessness of his madness. She had saved it out of love, and he had not even—but no—there was a new memory there—love he had for her, passionate, tender, true, a love that had not its place among the terrors of the past. But—was not this a new dream, a new delusion of his shaken brain? And if he loved her, was it not yet more terrible to have deceived the loved one, more monstrous, more infamous, more utterly damnable? The figure of her rose before him, pitiful, thin, weak, with outstretched hands and trusting eyes—and he had taken of her all she had. Neither heart, nor body, nor brain could bear more.

"Vjera! God! Forgive me!" With the cry of a breaking heart the poor Count fell forward from his seat and lay in a heap, motionless upon the floor.

Only his stiffening fingers, crooked and contorted, worked nervously for a few minutes, scratching at the rough boards. Then all was quite still in the little room.

There was a noise outside, and some one opened the door. The Cossack stood upon the threshold, holding his hand up against the lamp, for he was dazzled as he entered from the outer darkness of the stairs. He looked about, and at first saw nothing, for the Count had fallen in the shadow of the table.

Then, seeing where he lay, Johann Schmidt came forward and knelt down, and with some difficulty turned his friend upon his back.

"Dead—poor Count!" he exclaimed in a low voice, bending down over the ghastly face.

The pale eyes were turned upward and inward, and the forehead was damp. Schmidt unbuttoned the threadbare coat from the breast. There was no waistcoat under it—nothing but a patched flannel shirt. A quantity of papers were folded neatly in a flat package in the inner pocket. Schmidt put down his head and listened for the beatings of the heart.

"So it is over!" he said mournfully, as he straightened himself upon his knees. Then he took one of the extended hands in his, and pressed it, and looked into the poor man's face, and felt the tears coming into his eyes.

"You were a good man," he said in sorrowful tones, "and a brave man in your way, and a true gentleman—and—I suppose it was not your fault if you were mad. Heaven give you peace and rest!"

He rose to his feet, debating what he should do.

"Poor Vjera!" he sighed. "Poor Vjera—she will go next!"

Once more, he looked down, and his eye caught sight of the papers projecting from the inner pocket of the coat, which was still open and thrown back upon the floor. It has been noticed more than once that Johann Schmidt was a man subject to attacks of quite irresistible curiosity. He hesitated a moment, and then came to the conclusion that he was as much entitled as any one else to be the Count's executor.

"It cannot harm him now," he said, as he extracted the bundle from its place.

One of the letters was quite fresh. The rest were evidently very old, being yellow with age and ragged at the edges. He turned over the former. It was addressed to Count Skariatine, at his lodging, and it bore the postmark of a town in Great-Russia, between Petersburg and Moscow. Schmidt took out the sheet, and his face suddenly grew very dark and angry. The handwriting was either in reality Akulina's, or it resembled it so closely as to have deceived a better expert than the Cossack.

The missive purported to be written by the wife of Count Skariatine's steward, and it set forth in rather servile and illiterate language that the said Count Skariatine and his eldest son were both dead, having been seized on the same day with the smallpox, of which there had been an epidemic in the neighbourhood, but which was supposed to have quite disappeared when they fell ill. A week later and within twenty-four hours of each other they had breathed their last. The Count Boris Michaelovitch was now the heir, and would do well to come home as soon as possible to look after his possessions, as the local authorities were likely to make a good thing out of it in his absence.

The Cossack swore a terrific oath, and stamped furiously on the floor as he rose to his feet. It was evident to him that Akulina had out of spite concocted the letter, and had managed to have it posted by some friend in Russia. He was not satisfied with one expletive, nor with many. The words he used need not be translated for the reader of the English language. It is enough to say that they were the strongest in the Cossack vocabulary, that they were well selected and applied with force and precision.

Johann Schmidt was exceedingly wroth with the tobacconist's wife, for it was clear that she had caused the Count's untimely death by her abominable practical joke. He went and leaned out of the window, churning and gnashing the fantastic expressions of his rage through his teeth.

Suddenly there was a noise in the room, a distinct, loud noise, as of shuffling with hands and feet. The Cossack's nerves were proof against ghostly terrors, but as he turned round he felt that his hair was standing erect upon his head.

The Count was on his feet and was looking at him.

CHAPTER XII

"I thought you were dead!" gasped the Cossack in dismay.

There was no answer. The Count did not appear to hear Schmidt's voice nor to see his figure. He acted like a man walking in his sleep, and it was by no means certain to the friend who watched him that his eyes were always open. As though nothing unusual had happened, the Count calmly undressed himself and got into bed. Three minutes later he was sound asleep and breathing regularly.

For a long time Johann Schmidt stood transfixed with wonder in his place at the open window. At last it dawned upon him that his friend had not been really dead, but had fallen into some sort of fit in the course of his lonely meditations, from which he had been awakened by the Cossack's terrific swearing. Why the latter had seemed to be invisible and inaudible to him, was a matter which Schmidt did not attempt to solve. It was clear that the Count was alive, and sleeping like other people. Schmidt hesitated some time as to what he should do. It was possible that his friend might wake again, and find himself desperately ill. He had been so evidently unlike himself, that Schmidt had feared he would become a raving maniac in the night, and had entered the house at his heels, seating himself upon the stairs just outside the door to wait for events, with the odd fidelity and forethought characteristic of him. The Count's cry had warned him that all was not right and he had entered the room, as has been seen.

He determined to wait some time longer, to see whether anything would happen. Meanwhile, he thrust Akulina's letter into his pocket, reflecting that as it was a forgery it would be best that the Count should not have it, lest he should be again misled by the contents. He sat down and waited.

Nothing happened. The clocks chimed the quarters up to one in the morning, a quarter-past, half-past—Schmidt was growing sleepy. The Count breathed regularly and lay in his bed without moving. Then, at last, the Cossack rose, looked at his friend once more, blew out the lamp, felt his way to the door and left the room. As he walked home through the quiet streets he swore that he would take vengeance upon Akulina, by producing the letter and reading it in her husband's presence, and before the assembled establishment, before the Count made his appearance. It was indeed not probable that he would come at all, considering all that he had suffered, though Schmidt knew that he generally came on Thursday morning, evidently weary and exhausted, but unconscious of the delusion which had possessed him during the previous day. Possibly, he was subject to a similar fit every Wednesday night, and had kept the fact a secret. Schmidt had always wondered what happened to him at the moment when he suddenly forgot his imaginary fortune and returned to his everyday senses.

The morning dawned at last, and it was Thursday. As there was no necessity for liberating the Count from arrest to-day, Akulina roused her husband with the lark, gave him his coffee promptly and sent him off to open the shop and catch the early customer. Before the shutters had been up more than a quarter of an hour, and while Fischelowitz was still sniffing the fresh morning air, Johann Schmidt appeared. His step was brisk, his brow was dark and his boots creaked ominously. With a very brief salutation he passed into the back shop, slipped off his coat and set to work with the determination of a man who feels that he must do something active as a momentary relief to his feelings.

Next came Vjera, paler than ever, with great black rings under her tired eyes, broken with the fatigues and anxieties of the previous day, but determined to double her work, if that were possible, in order to make up for the money she had borrowed of Schmidt and, through him, of Dumnoff. As she dropped her shawl, Fischelowitz caught sight of the back of her head, and broke into a laugh.

"Why, Vjera!" he cried. "What have you done? You have made yourself look perfectly ridiculous!"

The poor girl turned scarlet, and busied herself at her table without answering. Her fingers trembled as she tried to handle her glass tube. The Cossack, whose anger had not been diluted by being left to boil all night, dropped his swivel knife and went up to Fischelowitz with a look in his face so extremely disagreeable that the tobacconist drew back a little, not knowing what to expect.

"I will tell you something," said Schmidt, savagely. "You will have to change your manners if you expect any of us to work for you."

"What do you mean?" stammered Fischelowitz, in whom nature had omitted to implant the gift of physical courage, except in such measure as saved him from the humiliation of being afraid of his wife.

"I mean what I say," answered the Cossack. "And if there is anything I hate, it is to repeat what I have said before hitting a man." His fists were clenched already, and one of them looked as though it were on the point of making a very emphatic gesture. Fischelowitz retired backwards into the front shop, while Vjera looked on from within, now pale again and badly frightened.

"Herr Schmidt! Herr Schmidt! Please, please be quiet! It does not matter!" she cried.

"Then what does matter?" inquired the Cossack over his shoulders, "If Vjera has cut off her hair," he said, turning again to Fischelowitz, "she has had a good reason for it. It is none of your business, nor mine either."

So saying he was about to go back to his work again.

"Upon my word!" exclaimed the tobacconist. "Upon my word! I do not understand what has got into the fellow."

"You do not understand?" cried Schmidt, facing him again. "I mean that if you laugh at Vjera I will break most of your bones."

At that moment Akulina's stout figure appeared, entering from the street. The Cossack stood still, glaring at her, his face growing white and contracted with anger. He was becoming dangerous, as good-tempered men will, when roused, especially when they have been brought up among people who, as a tribe, would rather fight than eat, at any time of day, from pure love of the thing. Even Akulina, who was not timid, hesitated as she stood on the threshold.

"What has happened?" she inquired, looking from Schmidt to her husband.

The latter came to her side, if not for protection, as might be maliciously supposed, at least for company.

"I cannot understand at all," said Fischelowitz, still edging away.

"You understand well enough, I think, and as for you, Frau Fischelowitz, I have something to talk of with you, too. But we will put it off until later," he added, as though suddenly changing his mind.

The Count himself had appeared in the doorway behind Akulina. Both she and her husband stood aside, looking at him curiously.

"Good-morning," he said, gravely taking off his hat and inclining his head a little. He acted as though quite unconscious of what had happened on the previous day, and they watched him as he quietly went into the room beyond, into which the Cossack had retired on seeing him enter.

He hung up his hat in its usual place, nodding to Schmidt, who was opposite to him. Then, as he turned, he met Vjera's eyes. It was a supreme moment for her, poor child. Would he remember anything of what had passed on the previous day? Or had he forgotten all, his debt, her saving of him and the sacrifice she had made? He looked at her so long and so steadily that she grew frightened. Then all at once he came close to her, and took her hand and kissed it as he had done when they had last parted, careless of Schmidt's presence.

"I have not forgotten, dear Vjera," he whispered in her ear.

Schmidt passed them quickly and again went out, whether from a sense of delicacy, or because he saw an opportunity of renewing the fight outside, is not certain. He closed the door of communication behind him.

Vjera looked up into the Count's eyes and the blush that rarely came, the blush of true happiness, mounted to her face.

"I have not forgotten, dearest," he said again. "There is a veil over yesterday—I think I must have been ill—but I know what you did for me and—and—" he hesitated as though seeking an expression.

For a few seconds again the poor girl felt the agony of suspense she knew so well.

"I do not know what right a man so poor as I has to say such a thing, Vjera," he continued. "But I love you, dear, and if you will take me, I will love you all my life, more and more. Will it be harder to be poor together than each for ourselves, alone?"

Vjera let her head fall upon his shoulder, happy at last. What did his madness matter now, since the one memory she craved had survived its destroying influence? He had forgotten his glorious hopes, his imaginary wealth, his expected friends, but he had not forgotten her, nor his love for her.

"Thank God!" she sighed, and the happy tears fell from her eyes upon the breast of his threadbare coat.

"But we must not forget to work, dear," she said, a few moments later.

"No," he answered. "We must not forget to work."

As she sat down to her table he pushed her chair back for her, and put into her hands her little glass tube, and then he went and took his own place opposite. For a long time they were left alone, but neither of them seemed to wonder at it, nor to hear the low, excited tones of many voices talking rapidly and often together in the shop outside. Whenever their eyes met, they both smiled, while their fingers did the accustomed mechanical work.

When Schmidt entered the outer shop for the second time, he found the tobacconist and his wife conversing in low tones together, in evident fear of being overheard. He came and stood before them, lowering his voice to the pitch of theirs, as he spoke.

"It is no fault of yours that the Count was not found dead in his bed this morning," he began, fixing his fiery eyes on Akulina.

"What? What? What is this?" asked Fischelowitz excitedly.

"Only this," said the Cossack, displaying the letter he had brought from the Count's rooms. "Nothing more. Your wife has succeeded very well. He is quite mad now. I found him last night, helpless, in a sort of fit, stiff and stark on the floor of his room. And this was in his pocket. Read it, Herr Fischelowitz. Read it, by all means. I suppose your wife does not mind your reading the letters she writes."

Fischelowitz took the letter stupidly, turned it over, saw the address, and took out the folded sheet. Akulina's face expressed a blank amazement almost comical in its vacuity. For once, she was taken off her guard. Her husband read the letter over twice and examined the handwriting curiously.

"A joke is a joke, Akulina," he said at last. "But you have carried this too far. What if the Count had died?"

"I would like to know what I am accused of," said Akulina, "and what all this is about."

"I suppose you know your own handwriting," observed the Cossack, taking the letter from the tobacconist's hands and holding it before her eyes. "And if that is not enough to drive the poor man to the madhouse I do not know what is. Perhaps you have forgotten all about it? Perhaps you are mad, too?"

Akulina read the writing in her turn. Then she grew very angry.

"It is an abominable lie!" she exclaimed. "I never had anything to do with it. I do not know whence this letter comes, and I do not care. I know nothing about it."

"I suppose no one can prevent your saying so, at least," retorted the Cossack.

"It is very queer," observed Fischelowitz, suddenly thrusting his hands into his pockets and beginning to whistle softly as he looked through the shop window.

"When I tell you that it is not my handwriting, you ought to be satisfied—" Akulina began.

"And yet none of us are," interrupted the Cossack with a laugh. "Strange, is it not?"

Dumnoff now came in, and a moment later the insignificant girl, who began to giggle foolishly as soon as she saw that something was happening which she could not understand.

"None of us are satisfied," continued Johann Schmidt, taking the letter from Akulina. "Here, Dumnoff, here Anna Nicolaevna, is this the Chosjaika's handwriting or not? Let everybody see and judge."

"It is outrageous!" exclaimed Akulina, trying to get possession of the letter again.

"You see how she tries to get it," laughed the Cossack, savagely. "She would be glad to tear it to pieces—of course she would."

"I wish you would all go about your business," said Fischelowitz with an approach to asperity.

Akulina was furious, but she did not know what to do. Everybody began talking together.

"Of course it is the Barina's handwriting," said Dumnoff confidently. He supposed it was always safe to follow Schmidt's lead, when he followed any one.

"Of course it is," chimed in the insignificant Anna.

"You—you minx—you flatter-cat, you little serpent!" cried Akulina, speaking three languages at once in her excitement. "Go—get along—go to your work—"

"No, no, stay!" exclaimed the Cossack authoritatively. "Do you know what this is?" he asked of all present again. "Our good mistress, here, has for some reason or other been trying to make the Count worse by having sham letters posted to him from home—"

"It is a lie! A base, abominable lie! Turn the man out, Christian Gregorovitch! Turn him out, or send for the police."

"Turn him out yourself," answered the tobacconist phlegmatically.

"Posted to him from home," continued the Cossack, "and telling him that his father and brother are dead and that he has come into property and the like. What do you think of that?"

"It is a shame," growled Dumnoff, beginning to understand.

The girl laughed foolishly.

"I swear to you," began Akulina, crimson with anger. "I swear to you by all—"

"Customers, customers!" exclaimed Fischelowitz in a stage whisper. "Quiet, I tell you!" He made a rush for the other side of the counter, and briskly assumed his professional smile. The others fell back into the corners.

Two gentlemen in black entered the shop. The one was a stout, angry-looking person of middle age, very dark, and very full about the lower part of the face, which was not concealed by the closely cut black beard. His companion was a diminutive little man, very thin and very spruce, not less than fifty years old. His face was entirely shaved and was deeply marked with lines and furrows. A pair of piercing grey eyes looked through big gold-rimmed spectacles. As he took off his hat, a few thin, sandy-coloured locks fluttered a little and then settled themselves upon the smooth surface of his cranium, like autumn leaves falling upon a marble statue in a garden.

"Herr Fischelowitz?" inquired the larger of the two customers, touching his hat but not removing it.

"At your service," answered the tobacconist. "Cigarettes?" he inquired. "Strong? Light? Kir, Samson, Dubec?"

"I am the new Russian Consul," said the stranger. "This gentleman is just arrived from Petersburg and has business with you."

"My name is Konstantin Grabofsky, and I am a lawyer," observed the little man very sharply.

Fischelowitz bowed till his nose almost came into collision with the counter. The others in the shop held their peace and opened their eyes.

"And I am told that Count Boris Michaelovitch Skariatine is here," continued the lawyer.

"Oh—the mad Count!" exclaimed Akulina with an angry laugh, and coming forward. "Yes, we can tell you all about him."

"I am sorry," said Grabofsky, "to hear you call him mad, since my business is with him, Barina, and not with you." His tone was, if possible, more incisive than before.

"Of course, we know that he is not a Count at all," said Akulina, somewhat annoyed by his sharpness.

"Do you? Then you are singularly mistaken. I shall be obliged if you will inform Count Skariatine that Konstantin Grabofsky desires the honour of an interview with him."

"Go and call him, Akulina," said Fischelowitz, "since the gentleman wishes to see him."

"Go yourself," retorted his wife.

"Go together, and be quick about it!" said the Consul, who was tired of waiting.

"And please to say that I wait his convenience," added the lawyer.

Dumnoff moved to Schmidt's side and whispered into his ear.

"Do you think they have come about the Gigerl?" he inquired anxiously. "Do you think they will arrest us again?"

"Durak!" laughed the Cossack. "How can two Russian gentlemen arrest you in Munich? This is something connected with the Count's friends. It is my belief that they have come at last. See—here he is."

The Count now entered from the back shop, calm and collected, as though not expecting anything extraordinary. The Russian Consul took off his hat and bowed with great politeness and the Count returned the salutation with equal civility. Fischelowitz and Akulina stood in the background anxiously watching events.

The lawyer also bowed and then, turning his face to the light, held his hand out.

"You have not forgotten me, Count Skariatine?" he said, in a tone of inquiry.

The Count stared hard at him as he took the proffered hand. Gradually, his face underwent a change. His forehead contracted, his eyes closed a little, his eyebrows rose, and an expression of quiet disdain settled about the lines of his mouth.

"I know you very well," he answered. "You are Doctor Konstantin Grabofsky, my father's lawyer. Do you come from him to renew the offer you made when we parted?"

"I have no offer to make," said the little man. "Will you do me the honour to indicate some place where we may be alone together for a moment?"

"I have no objection to that," replied the Count. "We can go into the street."

They passed out together, leaving the establishment of Christian Fischelowitz in a condition of great astonishment. The tobacconist hastily produced his best cigarettes and entreated the Consul to try one, making signs to the other occupants of the shop to return to their occupations in the inner room.

"How long have you known Count Skariatine?" inquired the Consul, carelessly, when he was alone with Fischelowitz.

"Six or seven years," answered the latter.

"I suppose you know his story? Your wife was good enough to inform us of that fact, though Doctor Grabofsky has reason to doubt the value of her information."

"We only know that he calls himself a Count." Fischelowitz held the authorities of his native country in holy awe, and was almost frightened out of his senses at being thus questioned by the Consul.

"He is quite at liberty to do so," answered the latter with a laugh. "The story is simple enough," he continued, "and there is no reason why you should not know it. The late Count Skariatine had two sons, of whom the present Count was the younger. Ten years ago, when barely twenty, he quarrelled with his father and elder brother, and they parted in anger. I must say that he seems to have acted hastily, though the old gentleman's views of life were eccentric, to say the least of it. For some reason or other, the elder brother never married. I have heard it said that he was crippled in childhood. Be that as it may, he was vindictive and spiteful by nature, and prevented the quarrel from being forgotten. The younger brother left the house with the clothes on his back, and steadily refused to accept the small allowance offered him, and which was his by right. And now the father and the eldest son are dead—they died suddenly of the smallpox—and Doctor Grabofsky has come to inform the Count that he is the heir. There you have the story in a nutshell."

"Then it is all true, after all!" cried Fischelowitz. "We all thought—"

"Thinking, when one knows nothing, is a dangerous and useless pastime," observed the Consul. "I will take a box of these cigarettes with me. They are good."

"Thank you most obediently, Milostivy Gosudar!" exclaimed Fischelowitz, bowing low. "I trust that the Gospodin Consul will honour me with his patronage. I have a great variety of tobaccos, Kir, Basma, Samson, Dubec Imperial, Swary—"

While Fischelowitz was recommending the productions of his Celebrated Manufactory to the Consul, Grabofsky and the Count were walking together up and down the smooth pavement outside.

"A great change has taken place in your family," Grabofsky was saying. "Had anything less extraordinary occurred, I should have written to you instead of coming in person. Your brother is dead, Count Skariatine."

"Dead!" exclaimed the Count, who had no recollection of the letter abstracted from his pocket by the Cossack. It had reached him after the weekly attack had begun, and the memory of it was gone with that of so many other occurrences.

"Dead," repeated the lawyer sharply, as though he would have made a nail of the word to drive it into the coffin.

"And how many children has he left?" inquired the Count.

"He died unmarried."

"So that I—"

"You are the lawful heir."

"Unless my father marries again." The colour rose in the Count's lean cheeks.

"That is impossible."

"Why?"

"Because he is dead, too."

"Then—"

"You are Count Skariatine, and I have the honour to offer you my services at this important juncture."

The Count breathed hard. The shock, overtaking him when he was in his normal condition, was tremendous. The colour came and went rapidly in his features, and he caught his breath, leaning heavily upon the little lawyer, who watched his face with some anxiety. Akulina's remark about the Count's madness had made him more careful than he would otherwise have been in his manner of breaking the news.

"I am not well," said the Count in a low voice. "To-day is Wednesday—I am never well on Wednesdays."

"To-day is Thursday," answered Grabofsky.

"Thursday? Thursday—" the Count reeled, and would have fallen, but for the support of the nervous little man's wiry arm.

Then, in the space of a second, took place that strange phenomenon of the intelligence which is as yet so imperfectly understood. It is called the "Transfer" in the jargon of the half-developed science which deals with suggestion and the like. Its effects are strange, sudden and complete, often observed, never understood, but chronicled in hundreds of cases and analysed in every seat of physiological learning in Europe. In the twinkling of an eye, a part or the whole of the intelligence, or of the sensations, is reversed in action, and this with a logical precision of which no description can give any idea. It is universally considered as the first step in the direction of recovery.

The action of the Count's mind was "transferred," therefore, since the word is consecrated by usage. Fortunately for him, the transfer coincided with a material change in his fortunes. Had this not been the case it would have had the effect of making him mad through the whole week, and sane only from Tuesday evening until the midnight of Wednesday. As it was, the result was of a contrary nature. Being now in reality restored to wealth and dignity, he was able to understand and appreciate the reality during six days, becoming again, in imagination, a cigarette-maker upon the seventh, a harmless delusion which already shows signs of disappearing, and from which the principal authorities confidently assert that he will soon be quite free.

He passed but one moment in a state of semi-consciousness. Then he raised his head, and stood erect, and to the great surprise of Grabofsky, showed no further surprise at the news he had just received.

"The fact is," he said, quietly, "I was expecting you yesterday. I had received a letter from the wife of the steward informing me of the death of my father and brother. I think your coming to-day must have disturbed me, as I have some difficulty in recalling the circumstances which attended our meeting here."

"A passing indisposition," suggested Grabofsky. "Nothing more. The weather is warm, sultry in fact."

"Yes, it must have been that. And now, we had better communicate the state of things to Herr Fischelowitz, to whom I consider myself much indebted."

"Our Consul came with me," said the lawyer. "He is in the shop. Perhaps you did not notice him."

"No—I do not think I did. I am afraid he thought me very careless."

"Not at all, not at all." Grabofsky began to think that there had been some truth in Akulina's remarks after all, but he kept his opinion to himself, then and afterwards, a course which was justified by subsequent events. He and the Count turned towards the shop, and, entering, found Fischelowitz and the Consul conversing together.

The Count bowed to the latter with much ceremony.

"I fear," he said, "that you must have thought me careless just now. The suddenness of the news I have received has affected me. Pray accept my best thanks for your kindness in accompanying Doctor Grabofsky this morning."

"Do not mention it, Count. I am only too glad to be of service."

"You are very kind. And now, Herr Fischelowitz," he continued, turning to the tobacconist, "it is my pleasant duty to thank you also. I looked for these gentlemen yesterday. They have arrived to-day. The change which I expected would take place has come, and I am about to return to my home. The memories of poverty and exile can never be pleasant, but I do not think that I have any just reason to complain. Will it please you, Herr Fischelowitz, and you, gentlemen, to go into the next room with me? I wish to take my leave of those who have so long been my companions."

Fischelowitz opened the door of communication and held it back respectfully for the Count to pass. His ideas were exceedingly confused, but his instinct told him to make all atonement in his power for his wife's outbursts of temper. The Count entered first, and the other three followed him, Grabofsky, the Consul, and Fischelowitz. The little back shop was very full. To judge from the last accents of Akulina's voice she had been repaying Johann Schmidt with compound interest, now that the right was on her side, for the manner in which he had attacked her. As the Count entered, however, all held their peace, and he began to speak in the midst of total silence. He stood by the little black table upon which his lean, stained fingers had manufactured so many hundreds of thousands of cigarettes.

"Herr Fischelowitz," he began, "I am here to say good-bye to you, to your good wife, and to my companions. During a number of years you have afforded me the opportunity of earning an honest living, and I have to thank you very heartily for the forbearance you have shown me. It is not your fault if your consideration for me has sometimes taken a passive rather than an active form. It was not your business to fight my battles. Give me your hand, Herr Fischelowitz. We part, as we have lived, good friends. I wish you all possible success."

The tobacconist bowed low as he respectfully shook hands.

"Too much honour," he said.

"Frau Fischelowitz," continued the Count, "you have acted according to your lights and your beliefs. I bear you no ill-will. I only hope that if any other poor gentleman should ever take my place you will not make his position harder than it would naturally be, and I trust that all may be well with you."

"I never meant it, Herr Graf," said Akulina, awkwardly, as she took his proffered hand.

He turned to the Cossack.

"Good-bye, Johann Schmidt, good-bye. I shall see you again, before long. We have always helped each other, my friend. I have much to thank you for."

"You have helped me, you mean," said the Cossack, in a rather shaky voice.

"No, no—each other, and we will continue to do so, I hope, in a different way. Good-bye, Dumnoff. You have a better heart than people think."

"Are you not going to take me to Russia, after all?" asked the mujik, almost humbly.

"Did I say I would? Then you shall go. But not as coachman, Dumnoff. Not as coachman, I think. Good-bye, Anna Nicolaevna," he said, turning to the insignificant girl, who was at last too much awed to giggle.

Then he came to Vjera's place. The girl was leaning forward, hiding her face in her hands, and resting her small, pointed elbows on the table.

"Vjera, dear," he said, bending down to her, "will you come with me, now?"

She looked up, suddenly, and her face was very white and drawn, and wet with tears.

"Oh no, no!" she said in a low voice. "How can I ever be worthy of you, since it is really true?"

But the Count put his arm round the poor little shell-maker's waist, and made her stand beside him in the midst of them all.

"Gentlemen," he said, in his calmly dignified manner, "let me present to you the Countess Skariatine. She will bear that name to-morrow. I owe you a confession before leaving you, in her honour and to my humiliation. I had contracted a debt of honour, and I had nothing wherewith to pay it. There was but an hour left—an hour, and then my life and my honour would have been gone together."

Vjera looked up into his face with a pitiful entreaty, but he would go on.

"She saved me, gentlemen," he continued. "She cut off her beautiful hair from her head, and sold it for me. But that is not the reason why she is to be my wife. There is a better reason than that. I love her, gentlemen, with all my heart and soul, and she has told me that she loves me."

He felt her weight upon him, and, looking down, he saw that she had fainted in his arms, with a look of joy upon her poor wan face which none there had ever seen in the face of man or woman.

And so love conquered.